"Disabled Voices is magical—it is writing about disability that resists inspiration porn and tells the more complicated story of being disabled. It made me laugh and cry. It made me want to take to the streets in protest. But I also found community with people like me and those with other disability in its pages. A must read."
– A.H. Reaume, disabled writer and feminist activist.

"Not since Shelley Tremain's edited collection *Pushing the Limits: Disabled Dykes Produce Culture* (1996) have I seen an anthology that brings together disability fiction, poetry, visual art, and non-fiction within a solid grounding in intersectional movements for social justice. We need these stories and the spaces like *Disabled Voices* to create new narratives that imagine ourselves into Mad, Crip futures."
– Qwo-Li Driskill, author of A*segi Stories: Cherokee Queer and Two-Spirit Memory* (2016, University of Arizona Press)

"In a world sutured together by the myth of uniformity, *Disabled Voices* imagines otherwise. Herein lies a profound argument for plurality: there are as many bodies, abilities, genres, and ways of being as there are people. Finally: community realized through complexity and knowledge created by people who have for so long been effaced."
– Alok V Menon, trans writer and performance artist

# DISABLED VOICES

## ANTHOLOGY

Edited by sb. smith

Edited by sb. smith
Foreword by Leah Lakshmi Piepzna-Samarasinha
Cover art on this book is a composite image of Shelby Brown's "Tribute to Disabled
Artists and Revolutionaries" painting series. This work is not to be reproduced, sold,
or otherwise altered without the artist's express written permission. Shelby Brown and
sb. smith collaborated on image composition.
Cover design by sb. smith; Interior layout by RMP and sb. smith

Library and Archives Canada Cataloguing in Publication

Title: Disabled voices anthology / edited by sb. smith.
Names: smith, sb., 1993- editor.
Description: Includes bibliographical references and index.
Identifiers: Canadiana (print) 20190191449 | Canadiana (ebook) 20190191481 | ISBN
9781775301950
(softcover) | ISBN 9781775301967 (HTML)
Subjects: LCSH: People with disabilities—Literary collections. | LCSH: People with
disabilities,
Writings of, American. | LCSH: People with disabilities, Writings of, Canadian. | LCSH:
People
with disabilities, Writings of, English. | CSH: People with disabilities, Writings of,
Canadian
(English)
Classification: LCC PS508.P56 D57 2020 | DDC 810.8/09207—dc23

Printed & bound in Canada by Marquis Imprimeur Inc., Montreal, QC

ISBN: 978-1-7753019-5-0 (bound)

Rebel Mountain Press—Nanoose Bay, BC, Canada
*We gratefully acknowledge that we are located on the traditional territory of the
Snaw-Naw-As First Nation. This book was edited on the territory of the Snuneymuxw
First Nation. We give thanks for the use of this land, and pay respect to the traditional
histories and living cultures of the Snaw-Na-Was and Snuneymuxw people.*

www.rebelmountainpress.com

For all the beautiful weirdos of our community.
We're all welcome here.

## Access Considerations

The text in this book consists of sans serif fonts to increase accessibility for those with print disabilities. While not officially a large print book, the text in this book is larger than most standard print books.

An e-book version of this book is available online for purchase, and may be available for your local library to acquire upon your request.

Each piece of writing containing sensitive, potentially triggering content features a content note in the opening lines.

If you have further access needs that we have not met, please consider emailing your access need(s) to the publisher at: rebelmountainpress@gmail.com. Rebel Mountain Press may or may not be able to provide further access and doing so is at their sole discretion.

# Contents

*Artwork*

# Editor's Note
## by sb. smith

My first introduction to criplit took place not all that long ago. Back in fall 2017, I chose Leah Lakshmi Piepzna-Samarasinha's *Bodymap* in my Introduction to Publishing course to write my first ever book review on. I experienced a too-heavy-for-the-middle-of-a-university-semester catharsis from doing so, and my instructor (hilariously) changed every instance of the word "ableism" in my assignment to "able-ism" as if it was a word *I* had invented. Regardless, I found my own crip experience reflected in those pages and a part of me felt deeply understood for the first time in my life. It was like discovering a new language for everything I'd been feeling, experiencing, and wanting to say for years.

In the following semester, I took another publishing course that Rebel Mountain Press (the publisher of this book) visited to present their catalogue of books. They had just released their LGBTQIA+ anthology and had an Indigenous anthology already under their belts. Sitting at the back of class during the presentation, I daydreamed of a Disability anthology and wished for a place I could devour more types of criplit. Although some Disabled anthologies of strictly one genre exist, I'd never heard of an anthology of several writing genres as well as art. I thought to myself, *I'm a good editor. Why can't I make that book?* At the end of class, I approached Rebel Mountain Press with my pitch for *Disabled Voices Anthology* and the rest was history!

The title of this book simply came from a literal explanation of what the book is: voices of Disabled people. I never thought to change it from the working title of *Disabled Voices Anthology* because the last thing our community needs is more euphemisms or mincing of words. I felt the title needed to be a firm presentation of the book's contents and a means to bring its creator's Disabled identities to the forefront.

As a result, I've taken some flack over the title. I've had a couple of icky emails, but even more intentional mis-namings or screwed-up noses in conversation with people. I've had everyone from friends, family, and colleagues forget and seem confused or shocked when I mention "the book I'm working on." I'd be lying if I said all feedback has been negative, but the subtle ableism (that I, as a Disabled person, am highly-attuned to) around the reception to this book in my personal and working circles has been discouraging, to say the least. Thankfully, I found the group of writers and artists I worked with to put this together to be incredibly supportive, gracious, patient, and generous throughout this process. So many kind words were offered from several of the authors during the editing process, all at times they didn't know I needed them most. The ceaseless enthusiasm and excitement from others in the Disabled community has been energizing in moments of burnout. On top of that, the writing and art contributions offered by some of my favourite crip writers and heroes is beyond my wildest dreams.

Even more, the title—our title—is important because it means direct visibility for Disabled writers and artists. It means we are putting ourselves and our work into the world, intentionally and unapologetically. We are intending for our voices to be heard, to be recognized. For so long, work by Disabled people has been undervalued in literary scenes and the art world. It's been ignored or invalidated and I, for one, am sick of that. I'm tired of fighting for my work to be appreciated half as much as my abled peers, tired of fighting for an ounce of recognition within my academic and working circles. I hate seeing the brilliant work from my friends and others in our community not getting the accolades they so deserve. I'm sure many Disabled creators feel the same.

My natural response to this type of marginalization is to say "fuck that" and carve out a deep, impossible-to-ignore space for our work to exist free of abled influence or judgement. With that in mind, this anthology is not for abled people. Just like we do not exist to inspire the masses, neither should our work. Our inherent value lies in our existence, not our productivity, and our work is not compiled here to prove our worth to abled people. This is for us.

*Disabled Voices Anthology* might not cover every Disability-related topic, examine every possible intersection, or speak for *all* Disabled people, of course, but I'm confident in saying it does a pretty damn good job of at least some of that! With a total of twenty-eight writers and artists from America, Canada, and England, they're bound to be a fairly diverse bunch. With work on wide-ranging topics such as invisible disabilities, mobility aid use, abuse, ableism from strangers, identity, substance use disorders, late-diagnosed neurodivergence, inclusion, online activism, access and accommodation, gender, race, sex and sexuality, internalized ableism, hospitalization and institutionalization, memory loss, pain, and so on, I hope we can all find reflections of ourselves and our experiences within these pages. The work in this anthology brings me a swell of mixed emotions: some heartbreak and sorrow, some anger, a lot of joy, and even more pride. I'm anticipating many of its readers will feel the same way. I hope this book gives Disabled readers what they need, and that it will be a place to return to again and again for reminders of the solidarity in the experiences we share.

With love and respect,
sb. smith

# Foreword

by Leah Lakshmi Piepzna-Samarasinha

It's the damnedest thing being a Disabled writer or being a Disabled person looking for Disabled writing. There is just so much bullshit to claw through. You want to read writing that tells the story of the nuts and bolts of your ordinary, amazing, cripped-out life—or you want to write that writing. You want to go beyond the 101, to write the weird shit, the shit that only other Disabled people (sometimes) get, to write all the things being Disabled, Deaf, Mad, sick and/or neurodiverse or DID have taught you. You want to write Disabled stories, and read them, and have Disabled conversations. You want to talk to each other.

But when you try to get your work published, with rare exceptions, you run into the wall. The wall of ableist crap. The wall that can only understand Disabled stories as heartwarming, or tragic, or both. The wall that can't go any further than the bare minimum of Disability 101. Every single time I write something for an abled editor, they insist that "people in their readership won't understand" what the word ableism means, or what the word "crip" means (even though it's been around since the '80s.) They say, "We want something that will appeal to the majority of readers," assuming that none of their readers are Disabled. If you're a disabled Black or brown writer, forget it, you can be one or the other, but not both. And much of the existing Disabled writing is white, white, white, white, white, and often racist.

The thing is, we do it anyway. The writing, the Disabled storytelling and thinking and critique and poetry and conversation. As my comrade and friend, disabled Korean writer and movement worker Stacey Milbern, says: no one is coming to save us, but we continue to save ourselves and each other. And one of the ways we are saving ourselves is by co-creating a vibrant new world of Disabled, Deaf, sick, Mad and neurodivergent writing and cultural production, one that is far from white white white white white.

We are doing it in books, self-published and not, and we are doing it in blogs and websites and podcasts from Alice Wong's *Disability Visibility* to Price Ro's *POWER NOT PITY*. We "overshare" (not) on crip Instagram, Twitter, and Facebook. I get 98 percent of my autistic community from online communities where we're all hanging out, pounding out our thoughts via text in the most beautifully blunt and sensitive ways. When we do this, we honour and lift up our people who have been doing Disabled writing for decades: Laura Hershey to Raymond Antrobus, Meg Day to Mayzoon Sahir, Harriet McBryde Johnson to Leroy F. Moore Jr., billie rain to Audre Lorde, Cyree Jarelle Johnson to Eli Clare, tatiana de la tierra to Gloria E. Anzaldua. We insist that we are not new and that disabled literature has not always been the #DisabilitySoWhite of much organized disability studies. We have rich disabled Black and brown lineages of writing—whether those writers used the "d" word or not.

*Disabled Voices Anthology* is part of that. When I published my book *Care Work: Dreaming Disability Justice*, I got into a huge argument with someone who wanted to put it in the "Health" section and told me that "Disability Studies" and "Disability Activism" weren't real categories for books. Before that, I resisted the urge of one would-be publisher who told me I'd have to choose to represent myself as the one "leader/spokesperson" of the disability justice movement in order to get published. What I've always wanted for Disability Justice literature is the opposite: a Disabled future where there is a vibrant Disability Justice section in every bookstore and library, where the shelves are groaning full of disabled writers and where there is access to PDFs and audiobooks and zines.

*Disabled Voices Anthology* is a crucial part of our new and old traditions: not apologizing for ourselves or writing for the abled, not translating or making ourselves small, but an unapologetic, vibrant part of that krip literary future that is now. Dive in.

~ Leah Lakshmi Piepzna-Samarasinha

*Cripple Punk Portrait #23 by Michaela Oteri*

# Three-Legged Beast
by Eryn Goodman

*Content note: ableist taunting and exclusion, ageism*

*Clack-thump, thump*
*Clack-thump, thump*

In the distance you can hear the sound of the three-legged beast.
Three distinct footsteps all sounding in a row
From the creature who grew a new leg to stay standing on its own.

Legend has it, this wretch never did need the third leg
That it held in its hand every step of its way.
Two-legged folk pushed the monster away; deemed it liar,
outcast, outlier.

Whispers wrap around the lame one's ankles, tripping it
As laughter encircles it and it is reduced
To an ancient, attention-seeking animal no one understands.

No one understands how hard the three-legged beast fought.
No one knows the pain they're in.
No one believes the exhaustion they face
every.
single.
day.

All abled people see is the young teenage kid who, for some reason,
uses a third leg.
Abled people never see how scared they are,
Or how much bravery it took to leave their two-legged self behind.

Three-legged, cryptid people of this world are no beasts.
They are simply individuals doing what they can to survive
To live lives outside the mythos forced upon them.

For that is all that these accusations are,
And all that they will ever be.

Myth.

# Blasphemy

by Bipin Kumar

*Content note: ableism, profanity*

I'm trying to figure out how my mind works. Whatever mental illness I have doesn't really matter that much. Everything I have to say about it comes from research I've done on how my brain works. As a result, I seem to know a lot about how things will happen. I'll just observe a scenario and the whole thing will be mapped out in my head. I don't even have to talk to anyone. Life works in themes and codes and I happen to know the predictability of all of it like I'm Neo from *The Matrix*. The conclusion to all that is I must be a god. Is that insane? Probably.

The running theme of my life recently has been Indian aunties who think it's okay to say some bullshit about how God will fix my disability. Here's the thing, I have a serious anxiety disorder and it's exacerbated by my disability. Everything from not being able to hold a girl's hand anymore—I mean, I haven't been able to anyway because of anxiety but now I really can't—to thinking I can't have a daughter anymore because I can't be the father she deserves. I actually don't care too much, to the point that it scares me sometimes. Am I sometimes reckless to the point of it being dangerous? Yes. Will the recklessness kill me? I don't know yet because I'm pretty careful. Usually.

I was recently at a bus stop and some old Indian lady walked up to me. I saw her from the corner of my eye and I thought "here we go." She asked me where I'm from. *I'm from here, my parents are from Punjab.* She asked me what kind of disability I have. First red flag right there. Especially if it's only the second question a stranger has asked you. *It's balance,* I tell her. Not even a minute goes by and she said: "God will make everything better." Something along those lines, anyway. I mostly just dissociate so I don't have to deal with this kind of thing. The second they see me, a young person, and notice my walker, I must stop registering as human to them because I'm no longer useful or whatever. I was explaining this kind of treatment to my cousin because it's the reason I don't like being around my other cousin's grandmother. I can hear all the passive-aggressiveness between her fake niceties. But it's not just from Indian ladies. I get it a lot from old people in general and it makes me hate them sometimes.

Exercise is important for mental health so I go to the gym. One time at the gym, I went to fill my water bottle at a fountain that has two nozzles. This old man came up to use the same fountain, noticed me and asked if I need help. First off, hell no. I told him I'm good, yet he proceeded to try to help. Then he stared at me and said "good boy" as I closed the cap of my bottle. Creepy much?

The day after the water bottle incident at the gym, I was leaving an open mic and trying to find a cab. I saw an old Indian lady in a taxi, and I immediately mentally mapped the entire interaction. I got in anyway and got asked "Hello, young man. How are you? What's your disability?" It's always the second question, after all. I had just clocked out at that point, but still, she asked me if I understand Punjabi and what my background is. After that, she mostly talked to the driver and I didn't want to waste my brain power on her.

As she was leaving the taxi, she grabbed my arm and said the usual "don't worry, God will make everything better." I rolled my eyes. She leaned into the backseat.

"Let me give you some advice, young man," she said. "Use this as an opportunity to be better than other young people. You will remember me."

I wanted to scream in her face.

"First off, have you heard my music, have you seen my art, or heard me speak? I didn't ask you or God's permission," I'd say. "I'm already amazing because I'm fucking insane and I love it. Did God give me my brain? Maybe. But my beliefs in God are murky at best. And why would I remember you? I've been talking to people like you for a hundred years. You're like a speck of dust talking to the Sun. I'm a god. Who the fuck are you?"

# Cat days

by Aimee Louw

*Content note: fatigue flare*

Some days are cat days.
On the couch in a haze,
looking for ways to awake
awaken,
awoke.
Yet, head on the pillow,
instant scooped with a ladle,
swimming may be off the table.

Some days are cat days.
She lounges flat on the couch,
gazing out the window,
so do I
lie—on the couch,
on the phone when a love asks, "What have you been up to?"
I mumble and change the subject.

And the blinds are open
The windows could be opened
That would let fresh air in.
That would let fresh air in.

The cat jumps down to eat three kibbles.
I might go buy a few things or do some work I promised
someone else,
might do the textmessagepostponereschedulesorry story.
Some days are just cat days
I'm not mature enough to nap, yet.
A nap would be an admission of defeat.
I feel the urge to fight, yet it drags me
to sleepful wakingness,
sleepless wakeful-less,

wakeless sleepfulness?
Sleepwalking would paint too active a picture to describe
these days;
Sleep-waking would be deceptive in its action;
Wake-sleeping is the word.
wake-sleeping. wake-sleeping.

I'm not mature enough to nap, yet. So, I watch a show
on Netflix about thirty-somethings trying to work
grown-up jobs and failing, over-acting arms flailing.
I take a break, ambivalently scroll Vancouver radio jobs. *I could do that,*
*couldn't do that, could I do that?*
I get back to the show; a nap seems an admission of defeat,
a surrender or submission to an unloving domme,
who offers no aftercare
who you're with just because she's there.

Wake-sleeping.
Wake-sleeping.

When the sun has, unlike me, un-fightingly gone down,
the windows are closed and I get to sleep.
When I awake the next day
and feel like making coffee in the Bodum
instead of the instant that I can't stand,
I sense things might be turning around.
And if, after a few hours, I have eaten,
I will have already beaten yesterday's
need to lie down after drinking water.
I will make it to the pool today.
Laps will let the air in.

Celebration happens speeding in the space between sidewalk
cracks,
in arms linked around a beloved's.
Celebration happens between lines of M.I.A. lyrics,
*Live fast, die young, bad girls do it well,*
*Live fast, die young, bad girls do it well.*

Celebration is in every inhalation and acceleration,
shedding of a days-long winter coat.

As the cat lies at the foot of my couch-bed, gazing into the fire,
You may wonder, "Doesn't she tire of that spot?
Staring into that flame?"
No—she is busy with the tasks of self-preserving;
banking time for the future, repaying the past.

There are days in-between, there are days that last for 96 hours.
And when a love asks,
"What have you been up to?"
One day, I'll be mature enough to wake from my nap
and say "I had a cat day."

*Cozy Witch by Jessi Eoin*

Disability: Fibromyalgia, bipolar disorder
Gender: Agender

Pronouns: They/them
Sexuality: Bisexual
Romantic attraction: Aromantic

# Crip Body as Beautiful
by Kate Grisim

I want to love my body and on good days, I do. I love its non-conformity. I love how my toes hide and curl against each other, how gravity weighs them down.

How my chicken legs lack muscle but are covered in so many shape-shifting moles, how the one on my knee looks like an eye keeping watch over me. How my knees knock and bruise each other senseless. How I want to keep my leg spasming after working them hard just for the sense of relief when it ends.

How my hands curl inward when I'm anxious, like turtles hiding in their shells.

How the curvature of my spine is a concave swimming pool, my shoulder blades the diving board. How, if I had a back massage every day, I would never want for anything else. How my voice warbles and wobbles like I'm sputtering underwater, always chasing the next deep breath.

On bad days, I wish my body was not the punch line of a joke. That it was seen as a natural way to be, and live, just like everybody else.

On good days, every part of my body is a good thing. Why would I want to see what everybody else does in the mirror? My curves and bumps and twistedness make my body unique. My body is endlessly contradictory. It has graciousness about it, a sense of humour.

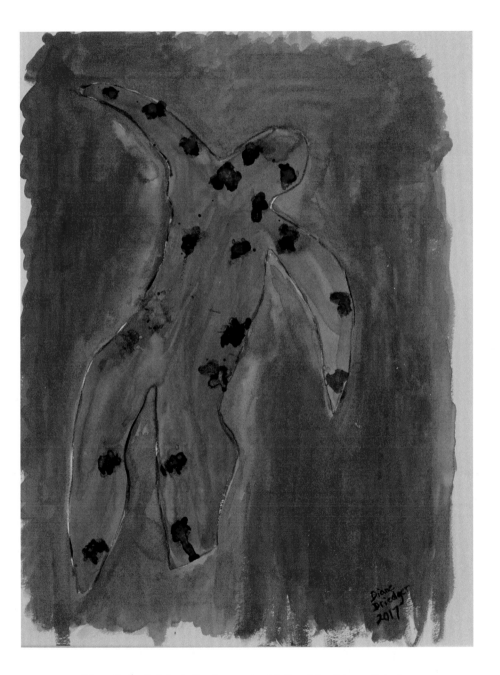

*Fibro Pain Points (after Icarus by Matisse) by Diane Driedger*

# The Falling Marionette
by Jennifer Lee Rossman

*Content note: physical rehabilitation, ableism, inspiration porn, brief mention of food, description of minor sports injury*

Stumbling and wobbling, her arms floating out from her body in the lower gravity of the clinic ship, Cass took her first steps. At the request of her brain, her hinged joints bent in sync, unsticking the gravity boot that locked her feet to the ship's deck. She set her booted foot down a few inches ahead and joy flooded her body.

And then, she panicked.

Too many moving parts, too many directions to bend. Bend a knee, straighten the ankle . . . Which way do the arms go?

The metal exoskeleton and lack of gravity kept her from collapsing like invisible strings holding her upright, but she folded gently in the general direction of the ground. She stared up at the puppetmaster who was not there.

"That's why we do this in orbit," her therapist said. "Hurts less."

He wrapped his hand around hers, all the little rods and pistons along his fingers curling with a precision she couldn't match. She stared at her own hand, thinking so loud she was surprised the other patients couldn't hear.

One by one her fingers contracted, squeezing with more strength than she ever remembered having, even before the spinal muscular atrophy progressed. Once she tried getting her legs under her, however, she slipped and slid like a baby deer on ice and her hand relaxed its grip. Her therapist had to lift her and wait for her knees to remember how to stand without buckling.

"But that was good. Try holding onto the bar this time for stability," he said.

Hold the bar? She could barely hold his hand.

Everyone stared. All the nurses and therapists and even some patients. Crowding at the edges of the room to watch the spectacle, offer too-enthusiastic encouragement, and mutter "poor girl" and "so brave" when they thought she couldn't hear.

Cass took another step and fell, tumbling sideways around the axis of the bar. She forgot how to let go.

~

There was a boy named Ahmed, a few years younger than Cass, who came into the clinic all mangled from an accident while she was recovering from her surgeries. A few months later and he was going back to Earth, his exoskeleton fully functional. He would still need to get used to the gravity, but he had been running and riding bikes while Cass was struggling to wiggle her toes.

She watched him stride out of the clinic with an ease she couldn't fathom, casually sidestepping a bunch of balloons while giving a thumbs-up to all the patients and staff who came to see him off.

"I'd be flat on my face if I tried that," she mumbled.

With a swipe of his hand, her physical therapist turned the window opaque. "You can't compare your progress to anyone else's. He started in a different place than you."

"But he started worse than me. Why does he get to be better sooner? Am I doing something wrong?"

His face made her regret complaining. So sad and annoyed at the same time.

"His injuries were quite severe," he acknowledged, sitting on her bed. "Shattered bones, torn muscles, damage to the spinal cord . . . Without the external and neural supports, he would have been paralyzed and possibly lost limbs. But his body took to therapy so easily because it already knew how to work."

Cass tried not to sigh or roll her eyes at yet another person explaining her own disease to her.

"Your brain works perfectly. So do your muscles. But the spinal muscular atrophy affects the way they talk to each other, so the messages don't get through so well." He pointed toward the window. "Ahmed's body already knew how to talk; we just taught it a new accent. Your body is struggling not to forget English and we want to teach it Mandarin and Hebrew."

Cass just looked at him, watching his fingers drum against his knee. Each gleaming metal support moved like clockwork, the joints springing and relaxing at every tug of electronic tendons. Did he even notice that he was doing it, or did it come so naturally that he didn't have to give any conscious thought to the process?

He followed her gaze and smiled. "You'll get there."

"Or maybe some of us just have more skilled puppeteers."

~

*It wasn't the fall that hurt you*, people said. *It was the landing.* Maybe in a physics sense, but not in her case. She'd been falling since birth. Falling behind the other babies and struggling to catch up to milestones. Nearly caught them for a while, using motorized chairs and machines that reached for things—before she was falling yet again.

First she couldn't lift her arms to feed herself, then she couldn't swallow. When her lungs gave out, they sent her to orbit for treatment. Less gravity pushing down on her chest kept her alive until surgery, but muscles atrophy in space.

She fell so far she needed marionette strings to pull her up. Miracle machines to save her life. She'd spent so many years falling, she didn't know how to stand up, but she had to learn because the worst part of falling wasn't the landing. No, it was people watching it happen.

The sad smiles, the stares, the being treated like less than human because she needed wheels and machines to get around. People talked slowly and used small words. If they talked to her at all. More often than not, they talked about her and over her.

*One step. Focus. All the joints pulling in different directions . . .*

When she got back to Earth, it would be different. She would walk. She would have value.

*Another step. Hold tight to the bar. Don't fall.*

~

Cass had forgotten how strong gravity could be. On the shuttle ride home, she felt her body sink into the seat, and it took more mental effort to lift her limbs. But her seat was just like everyone else's, no special supports or straps, and she could scratch her own nose without asking someone for help.

When they landed, she exited with everyone else. No ramp or

waiting for an attendant to unhook her chair. Just Cass, her brain and muscles finally working as they were meant to. Neurons firing, messages travelling along synthetic pathways to tendons made of pistons and actuators, pulling and pushing her joints like muscles should have.

She walked out of the ship, taller and happier than she'd ever been. Her legs moved stiffly, wobbled a bit, but her strings kept her from falling and she even waved at the crowd on the edge of the landing pad—who were not all there to see her, she realized as the other passengers went to hug their families. She let out a relieved breath and told her clenched hands to relax. No more spectacle or pity, just a human among humans.

At first, her parents didn't know how to hug her. Too much metal around her torso, not enough snuggly daughter to squish. But they hadn't seen her in months and the metal skeleton only held up their reunion for a few awkward seconds.

"You're taller than I am," her mother said with a laugh. She started crying.

Her father cleared his throat and tried to hide his emotions with humour as they walked back to their aerocar. "Glad it worked out for you, kid. I was worried they wouldn't refund the money I spent signing you up for hockey."

Hockey? Cass knew he was joking, but . . . sports? She'd never even considered sports.

The world opened up before her, full of possibilities. She could play sports now. Real ones, not the virtual kind where you throw a pixel ball with the flick of a finger. She could learn piano. She could visit that museum that didn't have a ramp! She could—

"Poor thing."

Cass froze. Her legs wouldn't budge, all neural activity being diverted to two little words. Her stomach felt like it would tumble out of her if not for the metal cage around her body.

She found the source of the comment: an old lady smiling sadly with her head cocked sideways. Her gaze travelled, eyes groping at every exposed support and lingering over the ones hidden by Cass' dress.

Cass opened her mouth, but choked on the tears that stung at her eyes and squeezed her throat.

*But I'm better*, she wanted to say. *These help me. I'm not something to pity anymore, and I never was.*

The woman turned to Cass' parents. "What's wrong with her?"

Her strings were cut, and Cass was falling again.

~

Surgeries, implants, and months of therapy, and Cass still lay in bed, afraid to be seen in public. Nothing had changed. If anything, this was worse.

Before, she needed the help everyone offered, opening doors and picking up dropped items. Not that they had the right to pity her for that, but at least she could understand their logic.

Now she was free, liberated by technology. A lump of wood finally given legs to dance on. But people saw her and they said "Oh, how awful. She can't ever be a *real* girl with those strings."

Her body almost killed her. She lived in space, she hurt for months, and she earned the right to walk and feed herself and braid her own hair. To be normal. But she would never be normal no matter how hard she tried. Always a freak, falling, falling.

A few months after leaving the clinic, she saw Ahmed on her vidscreen, winning every event in a sporting competition for Disabled people. Prerecorded segments told his story: Star athlete in high school, tragically mutilated when his aerocar fell from the sky with a malfunctioning thruster. *Look at how brave he is*, a voiceover said in a tone that definitely came from a tilted head. *Going through all those awful surgeries but never losing hope. He never gave up! So amazing!*

And now he was not only competing as a Disabled athlete, but advocating for Disabled rights and building wheelchairs for kids in the Congo. He was an inspiration. Not to Cass, but to all the reporters and announcers who had never had so much as a sprained ankle in their lives.

She tested her legs, running little laps around her bedroom and jumping hurdles made of kitchen chairs. Her puppeteer wasn't skilled enough yet, maybe never would be. Cass wasn't sure she wanted to be an inspiration anyway.

Were those her only choices? Keep to Disabled circles and let abled people find strength in the misery they projected on her, or try to integrate into the abled world only to have every person she met try and snip her strings?

~

Like a baby deer, Cass struggled to stand on the ice. Her body was not meant for skates, but the bulky hockey uniform hid the metal bars that ran along every bone. Her teammates were all "real" girls—no strings, no disabilities—and as far as they knew, so was she.

For weeks, Cass went to practice and taught her limbs to move in different ways than they ever had, and taught herself to trust. Pizza afterwards, laughter and fun with the girls. A glimmer of hope for a normal future, if only she could keep her uniform on.

Their first game found Cass with thousands of eyes on her, boring through the layers of pads and seeing every misstep for what it was: distraction making her neurons not fire strongly enough.

*Focus. One leg, then the other. Hold the stick tight.*

The puck came her way. She lunged, sent it skittering from the goal. Then, in the cheers and excitement, she lost her footing.

*Falling. Always falling.*

Her face hit the ice, her cheek splitting. She took off a glove to feel for blood as another girl skated over. Her hand curled around Cass', pulling her up. A glance at the exoskeleton, a friendly smile devoid of pity.

Cass wasn't falling anymore.

*Cripple Punk Portrait #19 by Michaela Oteri*

# "Transabled"—or, a Suicide Note from a Leg to a Body

by Isabella J. Mansfield

*Content note: body integrity identity disorder, brief mention of suicide*

there are people out there,
some sub
       sub
          subculture
who pay unethical doctors
to remove healthy limbs
from healthy bodies
disable them permanently
bring them to their knees
     or remove their knees entirely

they disfigure themselves in the name of—
nobody knows what. some idolization?
fetish, perversion, or alienation?
maybe they can't shake feeling "wrong"
to them, a complete body should be
in     com       plete
they long for physical absence
and they'll fight their emptiness
with ropes and tourniquets and knives—
anything to rid themselves
of this flesh without a soul

there is talk of mental illness,
for what else could it be?

they want what they can't have
they want what they don't have
what others have
on some days I worry
I am no different

my dead-ish limb
still bleeds, still feels
but hangs lifeless:
a shell of what it once was

what does it say of me
to occasionally wonder:

would it be easier to detach,
to remove its dead weight?

would it feel better
to feel nothing at all?

would I be regarded as one of them?
for feeling like part of my body doesn't belong
when it leaves me waiting for a suicide note it can't write,
               a farewell left unsaid
                    goodbyes dangling uselessly
                                   in
                         the
                                         air

# Walking Class

by Susan Mockler

*Content note: hospitalization, car accident, physical rehabilitation*

I set *The New Yorker* on the nightstand beside my hospital bed and checked the clock. I'd read for twenty-five minutes without my mind straying or my eyes growing heavy with fatigue. Twenty-five minutes? A new personal record.

I'd suffered a concussion in a car accident five months prior. The split-second impact of the car striking a moose made my head collide with the 1,500-pound animal as it hurtled through the windshield, snapping my neck. At first, the spinal injury had left me completely paralyzed from the neck down, but the doctors assured me that I didn't have brain damage. Yet, even as the function in my left arm returned, even as I was able to use my legs to propel a manual wheelchair, my thoughts still lacked clarity. Memories blurred and fragments from before the accident were lost.

But, I'd read for nearly half an hour! Maybe I *had* retained this part of my past life. Despite everything that had altered in my body, maybe my mind really was still me.

I double-checked the clock and realized my ex-husband Daniel would be visiting soon. We'd separated two years before the accident, but he'd been at my side since the injury. This surprised my family and friends, but not me. Ten years—a third of our lives—we'd grown up together, and it wasn't easy to let go. Besides, love had never been the problem for us.

He had been out west for ten days seeing his family and I had missed him. After staying in Ottawa with me all fall, my mother had returned to London, and my friends were visiting less often. Without Daniel there, I felt disconnected from life beyond the rehabilitation centre. Nobody there really knew me for *me*.

I wheeled away from the bed and crossed the room. Maybe I'd head to the elevator by the nursing station to wait for him. As I edged toward the door leading to the hallway, I heard the stamping of boots along the corridor and then Daniel burst into my room.

"Hello," he said, bending down to kiss my cheek. His face was ruddy from the cold, and his blue eyes flashed.

"Your lips are freezing," I said as I inhaled his crisp, clean scent tinged with wood smoke and pine. "How was your trip?"

"Great. Mom and Dad are good. My sisters are good. Everyone asked about you."

He whipped off his coat and settled into a chair beside the bed. I moved next to him, locking the brakes on my wheelchair. Daniel unzipped his gym bag and removed a video camera.

"I have some of our old tapes. I thought I could video you too, show them how well you're doing," he said.

"I don't—"

"Let's start with the videos."

Daniel turned off the overhead lights and flipped a switch on the camera. Images of me, Daniel, my mother, grandmother, and sister flickered on the wall in front of us. It was a video of my mother's house at Christmas three years ago. The sound was on, but I wasn't listening, transfixed by this former version of myself sitting cross-legged on the living room floor, tugging a thread from my cardigan sleeve, pushing strands of hair behind my right ear with my right hand. This was *me*, before everything fell apart. *Me* but not me.

"Daniel," I squeezed out as my throat constricted. "I can't watch this."

"Why?"

"Just turn it off. Right now," I said and wheeled to the light switch, obliterating the pictures still flashing on the wall with the harsh, bright florescent glow.

"What's wrong?"

I took a deep breath then exhaled slowly, making a shuddering, rasping noise.

"It's too hard to watch."

"I'm sorry," he said as he knelt beside me and took my hand. "I thought it would bring back good memories."

"I'm just . . . so different now. It's not *me* anymore."

I blinked back tears. I had to contain myself. If I started crying, I was afraid a terrible unhinging would occur. I was afraid it might never stop.

"You're still the same person," Daniel said.

"I'm not."

"You're getting better all the time. Look how far you've come."

"I just want to go to bed. Okay?"

"Sure," he said and stood to gather his things. "Can I get you anything before I go? Some water?"

"I've got some here. I'll talk to you tomorrow."

After he left, I picked up my plastic mug with my left hand and sipped water. I stared down at the rims on the wheels of my chair, at my right hand resting on my lap with its fingers clenched in a fist from involuntary spasm.

The next afternoon, I was in the workout room with Kyle, one of the physiotherapy assistants who was 31 years old like me.

"I hear you're going home soon," he said.

"Next week," I said. "But I'll be returning as an outpatient."

"You can't bear to leave all this behind?"

"Not yet."

"It's a big change but you're ready for it. Want to start with the footcycle?"

He attached the apparatus to the bottom of my wheelchair and strapped my feet to the pedals, then set the timer for twenty minutes.

"Be back in a bit," he said before crossing the room to set up weights for two young men in chairs.

I started to pedal. I loved the footcycle. It was like riding a bike and I could move my legs faster doing this than anything else. I focused on each movement: alternating legs, the upward thrust of my knee, the downward push of my foot against the pedal, powering the turning of the wheel. Again and again. The buzzer signaling the twenty minutes had ended surprised me, pulled me back into the room.

"Be right there," Kyle called.

He came back over and unstrapped my feet from the footcycle.

"Hey," he said. "Have you heard the new Alanis Morissette album, *Jagged Little Pill?*"

"The teen pop singer?"

"She's this angry rock chick now."

"Is it any good?"

"It's great. Some radio stations won't even play it because it's explicit." He glanced around the gym after detaching the footcycle. "If the crowd thins out, I'll bring in the boom box and play it for you."

Each afternoon from four to five p.m., the gym was reserved for "walking class" where patients could practice walking the thirty-metre length of the gym. A few chairs were set up in the middle for rest stops.

I parked my chair at one end. My legs were tired from the footcycle, so I waited a few minutes before starting. I sipped water and watched the others.

A tall, lean man sauntered beside his wife. He nodded as he passed by me. He was three weeks back in the world after a two-month-long coma. His body seemed to be functioning well—he stood erect and proud—but I wasn't sure about his mind since his wife did all the talking. On the other side of the gym, a few amputees strapped prosthetic legs to their stumps, and elderly men and women hobbled along, clutching canes and walkers. My people.

For the last five months they had all been my peers. There was safety here, everyone was damaged and everyone was the same. I belonged here, knew who I was, but soon I'd be on the outside. How would I manage? Who would I be?

I took up my cane and joined the procession. As I was nearing the end of my laps, Kyle hurried into the gym, holding up a music player.

"I don't think those two will mind hearing a few tunes," he said, nodding toward two women, maybe in their mid-eighties, shuffling across the floor on the other side of the gym, hands clinging to their walkers.

"This is my favourite," he said, inserting the CD and skipping one track. "It's called 'You Oughta Know.'"

The song began softly, almost sweetly, before the tone and instrumentation shifted and the music pounded through the gym. I marveled at the rage in Alanis' voice and the frank, sexual lyrics.

I glanced at my four-pronged cane standing on the floor beside me and at my wheelchair. Across the room, the two older women shambled along, oblivious to the fury, sex, and betrayal that echoed off the walls. I giggled that it was here, in the gym of the rehab centre, that I was hearing this song for the first time. The more I thought about it, the more I laughed.

I laughed with pleasure. I laughed with relief. I gasped for air, tears streamed down my cheeks. I laughed a full, throaty, bodily laugh. The kind of laugh I thought I'd never laugh again.

*Cripple Punk Portrait #21 by Michaela Oteri*

# HASHTAGGETLOUD

by Jill M. Talbot

*Content note: institutionalization, hospitalization, substance use, brief mention of rape, mention of sex work, description of shock therapy*

Note: A record for reference in the case of Patient X. Some names have been redacted for confidentiality.

Once upon a time in a psych ward far, far away lived a girl with a lobotomy who became an artist. This is how I wish you started your article on "mental illness" and art, referencing the latest show at the art gallery where someone apparently vandalized the entrance.

What does any of this have to do with being sad? Am I maybe just a psychopath with no feelings at all? Maybe a little bipolar with a tinge of warrior gene? Maybe I sold my soul to the devil? Maybe Emily Carr didn't accept my application and now I just go making graffiti in bathrooms with heroin smoke?

What, you've never had a taste of down? Think only proper sophisticated people do morphine with a glass of chardonnay? Think maybe I have a little bit of brain damage from the ECT? Or maybe you think I should just cut off my ear like Van Gogh and then I could get a seat at the real people table. Maybe I'm just jealous. Are eagles jealous of seagulls because there are more of them? Maybe I just don't have the attention span for *Infinite Jest*. Maybe I was dropped on the head as a child.

You really want us crazies to #GETLOUD for mental health? #GODSAVEME? Who got loud last year? You all just want to feel good about yourselves, so you can go home to your chardonnay and your fucking shih tzu and family portrait of three future junkies with missing teeth and a frame that says your family name with a little happy face emoji next to it to remind you how you should feel. At least I *know* how to feel. #iQuit. #NewiPhoneOutNextSeason! #GETLOUD is pretending to care about you—first come, first serve! Get your pencil baptized here!

I seen more hope in a soup kitchen. And don't tell me how brave you were to once walk through that place or how you once gave a crying girl in fishnet stockings a bus ticket and an AA brochure. Don't tell me how you lock your car doors and pray. Or do. At least that would be honest.

I know, I know. You think I seen *Fight Club* too many times and nobody loved me as a child and boohoo. You want a sad story? A really sad story? A fucking cry-your-eyes-out-and-find-Jesus-story? Maybe you want to be the next celebrity who goes homeless for a night and gets five billion Facebook shares for the courage to sleep next to us without even paying for it. Maybe you want to bring your kids here to say, *Hey, kids, don't do drugs!* Don't, by the way.

Fuck you. I'm getting to the sad story, I just wanted to work you up a bit first.

In the hospital, they put me in restraints spread eagle, sweat made the gown stick to me, and I screamed but they wouldn't even let me go to the bathroom. People stared like I was the apocalypse.

*What did you take?* they asked.

*I took the art*, I said. I took the red pill. I took the apocalypse. I took all your sins and look what they've done!

*Bipolar*, they said after they decided I wasn't just a crack addict.

They gave me enough drugs to put me in a coma and forget about the art. I'm bipolar so naturally I'm supposed to be an artist. Let me tell you, in the hospital, everyone's an artist. In the gutter, anyone can be a genius. I am fucking Picasso. I am Jesus. Take an Instagram of that grilled cheese. Form a new committee for the enlightened. Get there for your mental wellness sit-ins. Make all your *You Are Not Alone* posters in your local art class and finger-paint a heart on your forehead. Go ahead, I won't stop you. Go right ahead.

So, after I escaped being committed, I spent some time in and out of shelters where PattyCake, who sold himself for a Polaroid camera when he was 16, and I would wander around the hipster cafés and the Downtown Eastside where a bitch beat me up because she thought I was her cousin and camera crews came to do documentaries on the art of the homeless as if their four-year-old had just finger-painted a middle finger and ███████ came to do his solidarity-with-the-homeless-youth benefit concert and everyone thought he was a hipster god for sleeping with us without paying and looking homeless when he probably lived in a fancy condo with a pretty hipster girlfriend who probably was a barista at the hipster café where the people are the art and I got arrested for the crime of existing.

*The people are the music?* PattyCake asked when we seen ████.
*The people are the vomit,* I said.

PattyCake took a picture and said, *Princess Kat, $2000.*

I said, *I've already been sold—hold me. I'm a fucking fraud.*

I was weak. Everyone always is the morning after. Today feels like the decade after. Don't you all know that the apocalypse already started? Haven't been Keeping Up with *The Leftovers*?

(Fuck you. I'm homeless, I can still Keep Up with your HBO references, your poverty porn Sundays with the cast of *Shameless* on Showcase or *Who Wants To Be a Douche* on the Cartoon Network.)

I curled up in fetal position and told PattyCake, *I don't want to be art. I don't want to be one of Lincoln Clarkes' whores. I don't want to be pennies in a wishing fountain. If people really thought their wishes would come true, they would throw toonies. I don't want to be a methadone bottle on a Christmas tree. Hold me. I don't care where we are, I want to be held.*

*PattyCake, PattyCake, baker's man, roll me a joint as fast as you can, roll it . . .* I would say.

They give you two options: Morally or mentally unfit, or unfit to have children. Unfit for art. So I took the art. I did an installation in Science World and was arrested for it. ████ and I flashed tourists and did anyone give us a grant?

*In the trauma centre, they have a safety evacuation plan for bomb threats,* PattyCake told me. *Is that supposed to make me feel safe?* he asked. I told him that he should feel whatever made him the opposite of ████. He should feel like a fucking piñata if he wanted.

Patty also told me that the more loaded on coke he was, the more money he would get from sad mothers with empty nest syndrome who went to church on Sunday while their husbands were off with their secretaries. With girls it's the opposite, we get daddy figures. #FreudWuzHere.

Then they decided that bipolar wasn't enough, I obviously also had to have a sick personality. I had one too many meltdowns for them to be classified as meltdowns and had to be classified as a lifestyle. But at least my lifestyle doesn't involve wearing yoga pants or praying for that stupid kid I seen in Vancouver throwing up all over herself only to walk off with her head in the air like SHE were the art. (#ForgiveMe.) They told me that I had brain damage from bathrooms. I asked them if I also had cooties, that would explain a lot. So the gallery assistants put another red dot on my forehead. And I started writing on the walls with Sharpies, and I wrote on every You Are Not Alone poster I could find: *HOW THE FUCK DO YOU KNOW?*

I'm so sad I'm going to chop off my soul. I have no soul. Put *that* on a poster. You know what the saddest part is? I was less alone in the gutter than I am in front of you folk with your #GETLOUD campaign who want me to be as quiet as a mouse, with your art and your poetry and your hypocrisy.

PattyCake was raped for being a fag and I actually started to miss the art where I could be his faghag and he could be my PattyCake. And everything would be okay because we would write graffiti on the walls of the café bathrooms that everything was okay. Also that ████████ is a douche and some other stuff. And we would take Polaroid pictures. And I would do my best to avoid hospitalization or jail where they would try to break me like a piñata. At least on the street you know who you are.

HashtagGarbageDay#GarbageDay.

PattyCake found civilization and now has a job where he guards the art. He deleted and blocked me from Facebook, but I seen him in his little "Nazi" uniform when I was looking for a restroom. He pretended he didn't even see me. So I left a Polaroid camera at his feet and watched him try to pretend he wasn't guarding his soul. His fingers started to twitch like he was going to roll a joint.

*For Adam by Ciro di Ruocco*

# Bed eight, the ER, 2am

by Hannah Foulger

*Content note: hospitalization, brief mention of IV and blood/veins,*
*mention of death and seizures*

Papery hands, bandaged eyebrow.
An IV, blood-tipped, siphons life
juice into my vein.
I have been alone forever
for three hours.

A man walks past
wearing five blankets.
He knows the best thing
about the hospital
is the blanket warmer.

My curtain, half open,
reveals the contentions of malaise:
ever beeping, hampers rolling,
two men grip their beds,
retching
as on New Year's Day.
No one has looked at me
for two hours. I am a ghost
with sufficient blood pressure.

I will not die tonight
but I may yet wither,
dry out like an old sponge,
forgotten
until my finger clip falls off.
Monitors scream for an hour.
A nurse adjusts,
removes my IV and never returns.

When I am allowed to stand and dress
a distant PA crackles
*terminal clean, bed ten.*

I have been wrong
about many things
but a terminal clean
does mean someone died.

Still, the only thing
that separates
bed eight
from bed ten
is bed nine.

In retrospect,
my head has an affinity
for hardwood and tile,
or the seizures do.

I had three the week you cut me out,
before I knew what they were.
And when each was over,
I heard your words in my mind,
as if for the first time, over again.

You are a broken blanket warmer in a drafty ward.

# Dear Wheels:
# A Letter of Thanks to My Wheelchair

by Rebecca Johnson

*Content note: ableism and internalized ableism, mention of inspiration porn*

Dear Wheels,

You help me move freely in this world and soar to the highest peaks, but why can't others see how you help me fly? Instead, they see a woman in a chair who needs help with every single thing in her life. In reality, you give me the independence to rise above that ignorance and know that I am capable and eager to live my life to the fullest.

While other parents taught their infants to walk, mine patiently taught me how to use my hand to direct you. I would win races against other children who did not see the difference between their running and my moving. My childhood friends didn't even notice you. They only saw a girl who was fun to play games and dolls with.

As a teenager, I started to hate you for you scaring the boys away. They would only pay attention to the wheels, not the girl who had a crush on them. I hated you for pushing them away, making them disgusted at how different I was from all the other girls. If only I was not tethered to you, if only I could walk, then I would have a boyfriend too and the rest of my life would be easy, right? Even though I directed all my hatred at you, you still rolled me forward and never left me helpless. You took me across the stage to graduate high school and then rolled me into adulthood.

I liked you again in college. You waited patiently as I was stationary at the computer desk with my studies. You understood that we would not go anywhere in this country as a Disabled woman without a secondary education. So, we went across the stage together again twice more, shocking the crowds and receiving loud cheers because we inspired them. But we didn't do it to inspire others. We did it out of necessity to survive in a world that looks only at the aid, not the person sitting in it.

We became one during those years, ignoring crushes and doing what was cool. I was never ashamed of you as people stared at us in public, prayed over us without approval, or took pity on my life. You empowered me to ignore those who didn't understand and to keep going forward in life.

Now, we live a full life. You get me to work where I counsel those who are able but discouraged by their normal struggles. Then, you get me to the classroom to teach freshmen in college. They say, "those who can't, teach," but I definitely *can* because of you!

After work, you bring me home to a man who loves me, wheels and all, and parents who would give their lives so my own would flourish. I love my life and it is only possible because of how I move with you.

Thank you,
Your loving passenger

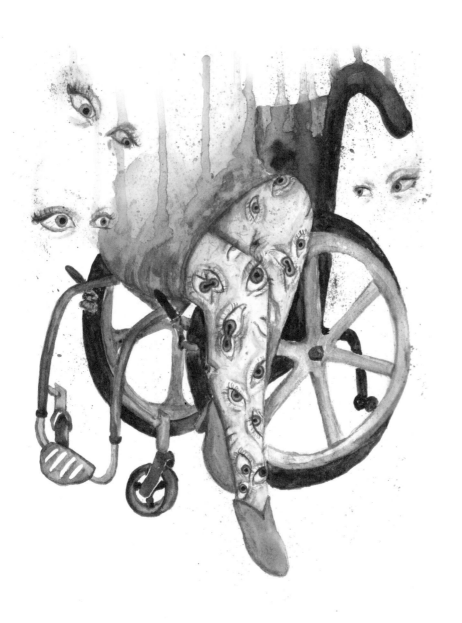

*All Eyes on Me by Eryn Goodman*

# The Invisible Girl

by Nicola Kapron

*Content note: internalized ableism*

The worst thing about having an invisible disability is not realizing you have it. I was first diagnosed with face blindness at the age of five or six, when my mother grew suspicious of my bone-deep certainty that wearing a wig for Halloween would make me unrecognizable to my friends. To me, the logic made perfect sense: I relied on hair and clothes to recognize people, so everyone else must have been doing the same. Even today, I still find myself thinking that way. Assumptions born from personal experience are difficult to shake.

One diagnosis led to a second, a third, and a fourth. My assumptions only built higher as I faced more academic pressure. I didn't take notes in class because it made my hand hurt, I consistently messed up calculations and word order, and I got lost easily during social outings. A negative pattern was beginning to emerge: I heard phrases like "you're being careless," "you just need to focus," and "you should be able to do this" so often that, years later, I'm still telling them to myself.

Well, guess what? I can't catch every mistake I make when I'm transcribing things, or doing math, or even just writing. It's not because I'm not trying, but because there's something wired differently in my brain that moves things around in the space between looking at a sentence, a word, a number, and copying it to another medium. Accompanying this coding difficulty are face blindness, which leaves me unable to recognize my own parents; topographagnosia, which keeps me from finding my way around; and dysgraphia, which makes handwriting an exercise in pain tolerance.

I was medically diagnosed with all four of my conditions around the age of twelve but I still have difficulty thinking of myself as "disabled" even now that I'm of university-age. It's not a matter of prejudice against Disability as an identity—at least, I don't think it is. I just don't feel qualified to take that word and apply it to myself. I'm not in a wheelchair. I have all my limbs. My senses are functional, even above-average in some areas. I'm able-bodied by any stretch of the word. How, exactly, do a few minor disconnects in my brain qualify as a disability?

Maybe I'm Disabled because my diagnoses have such a big impact on me that I have to plan my whole life around them. I'm scared to leave the house because I know how easily I get lost, so I go out of my way to avoid social events. If I have to go, I don't go alone, and I make sure my phone is fully charged in case I have to find my way back with Google Maps. I'm scared to talk to people because I know I won't recognize them later, so I don't approach people, not even my close friends. After all, when you regularly confuse complete strangers for your family members, you can't afford to walk up and start talking to someone.

When I was younger, I was scared of school because I knew I would have to write all my notes by hand and I just couldn't keep up. For most of middle school, I wrote almost nothing in my binders, relying on my memory to carry me through. That technique worked better than it had any right to.

When I entered high school in the wake of a friend with similar disabilities, our families fought to get me permission to use a laptop in classes; first a school-provided computer, then my own personal device later on. I didn't understand the importance of this accommodation until I experienced it. I could take notes again. I could start working on my assignments during my lunch break or even while they were still being explained. I could show the teachers exactly what I was working on and what my questions were. For the first time in ages, school was fun. All it took was a piece of assistive technology.

A few years later, I had a similar experience when I began to use GPS and bus-tracking apps to navigate. The world suddenly seemed so much larger, so much more open. I could travel across town on my own which opened the door to job opportunities, outings with friends, and solitary day trips—all things I would normally have to rely on someone else for. I haven't found anything to help me recognize faces yet, but if I ever do, I fully expect to experience the same exhilarating shift as my universe rearranges itself.

People experience many kinds of invisibility in this world. The most consuming, I think, is the act of trying to pass for normal. I dedicated years of my life to this fruitless pursuit, desperately trying to convince others that I didn't need help. That I wasn't struggling. That I wasn't missing out on what life had to offer. Now, I've finally begun peeling back the masks of normativity, which were uncomfortable and stuffy and never fit me properly anyway.

Here's what I've learned from twenty years of living with multiple invisible disabilities: I am Disabled. I'm going to fight for my access needs. I don't want to be invisible.

# Storage

by Niamh Timmons

*Content notes: medical research/experimentation, mention of transphobia, chip implantation, profanity*

I went through a series of meeting all the staff at the hemophilia clinic in my town. Flexed my joints for the physical therapist, talked to the hematologist about new medicines, had blood drawn, and then a social worker would check in.

The social worker was the least weird of them all about me being Transgender. She wanted to know how I've been doing over the past year. Most of my responses were from a canned script, with some vulnerabilities sprinkled in to get a little compassion out of her. I just wanted to be done and out of there. The social worker routed the conversation to potential resources.

"Would it be okay with you if I connected you with a Zanith representative? They have a program that might be able to help you financially. One of the reps is actually already here talking to another patient. I wouldn't do so without your permission, of course," she said.

"Could you tell me more about the program?" I asked. It wasn't unusual to hear about a company doing a study or survey or collecting medical data and giving some sort of cash compensation. I hadn't heard of Zanith before though.

"I'm not too sure of the details. I believe it's a monthly check-in where they collect data. They offer some monetary compensation for your time. I remember you saying that you were just released by your employer—"

"I was fired for being Trans."

"Right . . . well, it could be good for your situation."

I let out a sigh. "Sure. I'll talk to the representative. It couldn't hurt, at least."

"Great. I'll let him know," she said while walking toward the door. "Thanks for your patience, Marceline. I know you'll make it through. Just make yourself comfortable." She smiled then turned around to leave.

The clinic room had barren white walls, a cheap looking bed I was sitting on, a desk, and standard medical equipment. There was a plastic magazine rack on the wall, most of them being hemophilia magazines. Lots of white boys running around while their parents watched. I brushed some crumbs from pizza I ate before the appointment off my skirt when someone knocked on the door.

"You can come in," I said.

"Hi, I'm Hank, the Zanith rep," he said, firmly shaking my hand before taking a seat across from me. "Your name is . . . " He lifted his clipboard up and squinted at the paper. "Marceline, correct?"

I nodded.

"Great! Now, I just wanted to talk about this special opportunity we have. Zanith doesn't normally work with hemophiliacs, but this new research project we've been developing is of special interest to the hemophiliac community. Your situation offers us an exciting opportunity to get more nuanced data."

"Um," I said. "What do you mean by 'nuanced data'?" I asked, making air quotes with my fingers.

"Well . . . there's no reason to beat around the bush. As I mentioned, we are interested in working with hemophiliacs—you fit that pool, certainly—but also Trans women," he said.

The words "Trans women" sounded rehearsed, as if his script covered up what he really wanted to say.

"These two particular variables are really enticing for the scope of this project."

Of course they're interested because I'm Trans. I didn't say anything as I thought about what he meant about "variables."

"We are offering a monthly stipend as well as insurance coverage for the rest of your life as compensation for being a participant in the project."

"Wait . . . what?" I asked. "What *is* this project?"

"Right. The important part," he started. "Zanith researchers have basically come to a conclusion it's too difficult to extract data from living subjects. Instead, they've determined it's better to work with cadavers. The trick is how to recruit potential subjects. Now, we're not asking for the results now. In fact, that would wreck the data that we want. Instead, we establish agreements for potential clients to have them give us their bodies after their death. In exchange, we offer compensation so you live comfortably."

I looked at him in shock.

"I understand your reaction. It's a lot to hear," he said and gave a chuckle. "I have a brochure so you can read up and get back to us about your decision. Feel free to take your time to think this over."

He pulled out a yellow brochure and handed it to me. The front had an old white woman with white curly hair. There was red text above her that read "Donating Your Body to Science".

"I should mention one last thing that's not covered in the brochure. Even though the best data comes from cadavers, we still like to do regular monthly monitoring to see how your body responds to different scenarios." He turned his head to the left and pointed to a golden microchip implanted behind his ear.

"I'm sorry," I shook my head. "This a lot to process right now."

"No problem. Of course. Take your time," he said as he stood up and shook my hand. "It was nice to meet you—Marcy, was it? Take care." He walked out of the room, closing the door to leave me sitting by myself. I looked down at my skirt and saw a tomato sauce stain from where I dusted off the crumbs. I sighed, got my stuff together, and left.

~

I spent a week or so mulling over the idea of participating in the Zanith project. My last pay cheque was deposited the week before, and it was enough to cover rent but it only left me with $20 to buy groceries for the month. I didn't really feel up to applying for another job but I needed money.

*Why not?* I thought to myself. *It doesn't matter what happens to me after I'm dead. And I* need *that money.*

I opened up my laptop and began an email to the address listed in the brochure.

> *Hello,*
>
> *My name is Marceline. Hank, a Zanith representative, talked to me about the hemophilia research opportunity. I needed some time to think it over but I would like to participate in*

*the research project if it's still an option. How much was the stipend?*

*Thanks,*
*Marceline*

It was only a few minutes before I got a reply. They needed some personal and banking information from me to process the stipend and then we scheduled an initial session. They provided an overview of what to expect at the first appointment. I replied with my availability, setting the appointment for later in the week.

~

The Zanith clinic was this super sterile looking building on Capitol Hill. People regularly passed it, probably unaware it was a company that studied dead bodies. I went in through its tall, transparent doors, that slid open with a gentle but powerful glide. The lobby was mostly empty save for some chairs alongside the walls. The floors were a marble white and looked as if they had never been dirty. I momentarily felt guilty for dirtying the floor with my years-old Dr. Martens. The guilt quickly passed though and I deliberately made a scuff mark on the floor as I walked to the desk.

I checked in with the receptionist and she gave me a clipboard with some papers to fill out. An assistant came out to grab me just as I finished the first page.

"Don't worry about finishing the paperwork right away," she said. "We can finish it in the back."

She opened a door next to the waiting area and led me back down another sterile hallway, then into a room that was also mostly empty save for something that looked like a medical reclining chair. The room had this blue tinge to it.

"My name is Frankie. I'll be working with you today. You were given an overview of today's session earlier, yes?"

"Uh, yeah," I said, thinking back to Hank at the hemophilia clinic and the email overview. "Something about a chip insertion and that's it."

"Right! That's it for this session. Now, could you come get on the chair."

I did so and reclined so I was lying on my back. It was stiff, but I shimmied to get somewhat comfortable.

"Actually, could you lie on your stomach? It's easier to do the insertion that way."

"Oh, sure thing." I struggled to flip over without getting off the chair. My chest started to ache as it pushed against the chair. It was stiffer than I thought.

"Now relax. The chip insertion won't take long, then you're free to go," she said while she swabbed the skin behind my ear with an alcohol pad. It tickled, but it's a sensation I'm used to from all my infusions for my hemophilia medications. "Now this is going to pinch and sting a bit."

Frankie pinched the little fatty tissue there is behind my ear. There was a sudden jabbing, and my whole body shook.

"That's the worst of it. Just need to make sure it's secure." She pinched more as she was tightening the chip into my skin. Then she stopped and my skin was still sore and aching, but the pain was mostly gone.

"That's it. You can sit up now," she said as she placed some instruments back on her tray. "Just finish up that paperwork and you should see your first stipend payout in your bank account later today."

I sat up and she took me to the door, pointing the way out to the exit. I went back into the lobby and filled out the remaining paperwork. The scuff mark I made earlier was gone. I wondered if the receptionist cleaned it while I was getting the chip inserted. My neck was still aching and I was trying to resist the urge to touch the chip. After finishing the paperwork, I handed the clipboard to the receptionist and headed out.

While waiting for the bus back home, I checked my bank account app on my phone to see if the stipend had arrived. Instead of a measly $20, there was $2,570 in my account.

"Fuck yeah!"

# Please Listen
by Deborah Chava Singer

*Content note: unsolicited medical advice*

I am not you,
your aunt,
the neighbour you once had.

I appreciate your concern,
desire to help,
good intentions.

But, this is not your body, not your disability.
You don't know my experience, body, history.
You don't know what has failed, has hurt, has helped.

So, please listen
when I tell you I know myself,
when I know what is true for me.

Thank you for your words
regarding my disability,
but I'd rather you listen to me.

# Eyebrows

by Cheryl Folland

*Content note: anxiety, sensory overload, compulsive behaviour, obsessive behaviour/fixations, trichotillomania, hospitalization*

*September 2nd*
My counsellor instructed me to keep this journal in hopes of identifying my obsessions and triggers. I think that it's utterly pointless and there's no merit in it. It's like whining into the void and I don't see how it will identify anything I don't already know.

I'm anxious. I have been anxious since I was a child. My mother used to scream in my face to shake me from my spiral. I would cry incessantly over something as trivial as a waiter bringing me pasta with the wrong sauce at a restaurant. Mother would yell "ENOUGH" in my face and I would dissolve into a silent puddle of obedience. It worked every time but now I am startled by loud noises.

*September 3rd*
I'm addicted to coffee. Not so much the consumption of it, but the comforting nature of a warm cup in my hands or the scent of the roasted beans mingled with heavy cream wafting from their place on my living room table. I'm also apparently addicted to treating this journal like a novel writing competition where I expound on the mundane using gloriously lavish language!

I set the coffee pot the night before with The Great Canadian Blend from President's Choice (because it's all I can afford and tastes more expensive than it is), a perfect hybrid of medium and light roast with notes of citrus and nuts. The blue glow from the LED interface cascades throughout the house in the early morning gloom to light my hazy path. I often forget to put my glasses on and kick a stray shoe. I smoke a cigarette and feed my cat, George, outside. I linger and give the cat gentle pets until the chime on the coffee maker rings three times. It's finished brewing and the morning is officially permitted to begin. The sun is not up, but my coffee is ready and my laptop is waiting.

I'm a creature of habit and endeavour to begin every morning this way. I sip creamy bitters from my sky-blue ceramic mug purchased from a local artisan market and set it on the table. I drink half of it and forget the rest until I arrive home from work in the evening. I'm always disappointed at my neglected mug, but I still fail to finish an entire cup every morning.

On the rare occasion I oversleep and cannot make coffee or I don't have cream, my day is ruined and I hate everything. I hate the bus even if it arrives on time because I have to be around people I don't know who ignore the "scent-free zone" signs and wear a bottle of dollar store cologne. I hate the rain even though I have a wonderful rainbow-striped umbrella with an automatic button that ejects it into the open position with one touch. I hate the way my favourite hat that keeps me warm feels like a cage for my head.

So, I try to never sleep in.

*September 8th*

Today, I drank an entire mug of coffee before leaving the house. Finally, I am not a failure. I also purchased a Venti Pumpkin Spice Latte on the way to work at Superstore just because I noticed Starbucks advertising them once again. This was another odd occasion that I finished an entire mug and I owe that entirely to it being half milk and syrup. The sugary-thick spiced cream creates a chug-it-all-now effect I could not resist. My teeth became gritty ten minutes into my shift and I jittered frantically like a hummingbird on too much sugar juice. My heightened heart rate invented social catastrophes out of ordinary encounters all while I became more efficient at menial tasks like using the iPod interface to shop customers' pick-up orders. I was able to shop 105 line items in under 28 minutes, beating my average of 65 items per hour. However, my administration and customer service became erratic. My emails to the front end department that handles refunds to accounts were full of typos and more than once I forgot to send an attachment. I stuttered words on the phone and, to my horror, in person as I tried, in vain, to communicate product substitutions and shortages to customers. My brain was operating faster than my mouth could keep up. I became fixated on correcting any errors in my speech pattern and kept customers waiting longer than the ideal five to eight minutes when they came to pick up their orders.

I blamed the coffee. In no way do I ever admit I suffer with anxiety in the heat of the moment. Nor will I confess my perfectionism that has me crying in the bathroom on my break for loading the wrong Karen order when two Karens were expected to pick up for the same time slot. I *should* have asked for a last name. I *should* have known better. Now, I will forever be seen as the idiot who loaded the wrong order. One little mistake sent me into a spiral and I was stuck on it for the remainder of the day. Like a snowball tumbling down a steep hill, the impact of my accidents—very literal accidents in the case of driving a cart into the automatic sliding doors to avoid colliding with a customer coming in the "out" door, thus knocking the very expensive door off its hinges and leaving me worried if they'll be able to lock the store at closing time—built until they collided with immovable force.

Then, the catastrophizing as I thought the store would inevitably be robbed in the night and I will be fired simply for failing to run over someone who disregarded the rules (which would have, in turn, also gotten me fired). I continued my shift mostly in tears or at least on the verge of them. Ten minutes before my shift was over, the store manager informed me they fixed the door five minutes after I broke it. But, all I could think of is how much of an idiot I must be and that I must do better to avoid driving a million-pound cart into anything regardless if the cart lacks brakes.

*September 11th*
Today at work, the store speakers were playing the same pop music they play nationwide that we've been listening to for three months. I've memorized the song order. It's a strange mixture of obscure '80s hits and last season's chart toppers. A co-worker decided to play me a new song they liked from their phone right when another staff member erupted into the room with an over-excited recounting of a scary soccer mom on the floor. I felt the hair on the back of my neck stand. My heart rate increased to the point where it felt like my eyes were shaking in their sockets. I couldn't make sense of the various sounds colliding in my ears. It was as if I was a drain and each noise was water pouring from several buckets, all competing to get into one drain hole. I felt submerged against my will and over my capacity and could not handle it. I placed both hands over my ears and yelled, "Too many sounds!" Tears poured out of my eyes and my arms began to shake in concert with the flip-flop in my stomach. They all stared

at me like I was crazy but thankfully became silent. My manager had entered the room at some point during the chaos and turned the volume down on the overhead music.

I blame the coffee.

*September 12th*
Dr. Harvey said coffee in itself is not my problem, but it is "exacerbating the underlying condition." She challenged me to fast from it for a time. I hate peppermint tea. And Dr. Harvey.

*October 4th*
No coffee for almost a month. I have no real excuse for why I haven't been writing—except that I don't want to. But, at this point, I can't make sense of the crap in my head and I've got no one to talk to.

When I stare at my fish tank, the fact that the goldfish poop has a weird thin casing on it allowing it to float about like a fecal sausage and the red platy poop does not, makes me wonder if fish care that they swim in ever-increasing toilet water. Why is it recommended to clean the tank only once a week? Why is it necessary to have a certain level of bacteria—from shit, no less—in the tank at all times? Is it safe to drink tea from a bag where a little staple holds the contents inside? Won't I get aluminum poisoning and end up with advanced Alzheimer's? I switched to looseleaf tea, but that is harder to clean up after I brew it and I'm certain I'll have to call a plumber soon to dislodge the fish-poop-tea-leaf-dam of doom that threatens to clog my drain. Inevitably, sewage will begin to back up and fill my bathtub because of my poor choice in pets and hot beverages.

Today, I pulled at a thread on my sweater, thinking it was harmless and better than tapping my foot so that my leg jiggles like a wiggly piece of J-ello held by a sticky toddler. I was *trying* to relieve my anxiety without anyone noticing, then a stranger on the bus pointed out there was a gaping hole in my left armpit. My face immediately flushed, and I pushed the stop request button a few stops too early. I ended up walking an extra 45 minutes home.

On the way home, I kept pulling at my sweater, the source of the day's awkward encounter, and ended up with a jean pocket filled with white lint and black yarn. My dryer must be broken, or about to die, with the amount of white lint that was on that sweater. I want to blame the poorly-manufactured sweater but more than anything I blame my inability to let things go. Like the way I spelled Jell-o before I looked it up on Google.

*October 5th*
My pulling on things has graduated to my hair. Not the way your older brother yanks on your ponytail causing you to fall on your butt in front of all his friends until they laugh every time you wear your hair up in their presence, but pulling like yanking out any hair that doesn't fit one by one. Today, the hairs that don't fit are rougher than the other ones. Almost like crinkle fries, they are wavy, coarse zig-zags. If I pull one out and that little protein casing on the end of the follicle doesn't come with it, it's a bust and I pull another until I'm satisfied. Sometimes this takes several tries. I can feel the tension in my body release as the entire follicle comes lose and the pores on my scalp are finally allowed to breathe.

*October 7th*
I made an appointment to see Dr. Harvey sooner than usual. I have a bald patch at the front of my head and all my socks have holes in them. Still no coffee, but I'm smoking more to try and do something else with my hands.

*October 8th*
Dr. Harvey says I have trick-o-lo-mania, or something like that. Apparently, it's very common in people with obsessive disorders. Comorbid was the word she used. I'm still not a fan of labels. I still rip them out of all my t-shirts. But I've cut my hair super short and started wearing a hat most of the time. My friends think I've gone alternative or something. Alternative to what exactly remains to be seen. Maybe I'll adopt the practice of wearing gloves.

*October 9th*
I picked up the medication that Dr. Harvey suggested I try in order to "curb compulsions." The alliteration in that phrase makes me so angry. Like, why does everything mental health-related have to come with a slogan. *Cipralex, curb your compulsions!* I'm not convinced that medication will work, but I also don't want to be irreparably bald.

I've learned through late night internet research that pulling out hair protein casings can often prevent hair from returning. That would make maintaining employment even more difficult than my bouts of staying in bed for a week do.

*October 10th*
Nothing new to report except that my forehead feels fuzzy from the inside. Like my brain is on a hotplate, the kind used for warming cups of forgotten coffee—I mean, tea—not the kind used to cook soup in a dorm.

*October 16th*
I made it an entire day without pulling my hair and then I decided to pluck my eyebrows. Now I'm on my way to the drugstore that's open until 10pm to find an eyebrow pencil close to my natural colour as possible. People with trich should not shape their own eyebrows. Note to self: hire an esthetician.

*October 31*
I am not obsessively or absently doing—what's the word for it—body repetitive behaviours. Makes me think of BRB. Like, I'll be right back after I do this alphabetized list of tasks:

    a) ask Mom how to make brownies
    b) buy butter
    c) clean the entire house (also in alphabetical order: bathroom, bedroom, compost, dishes, dusting, fish tank, floors, garbage, kitchen, laundry, litterbox, windows)
    d) drive to store
    e) eat something
    f) freeze while paying for parking
    g) get groceries.

Instead of BRB, I'm late. For everything. If I don't put a reminder in my phone for each task, one on my wall calendar, and on the back of my hand, I will be late. Sometimes I double book myself. Other times I don't show up. The nice side of this issue is I don't really care, but I am more worried that I should care.

*November 1st*
Yesterday was Halloween. Dressed up as my past self. Meaning, I wore yesterday's clothes. I forgot it was Halloween.

*November 2nd*
Dr. Harvey gave me the number for the crisis line again today after I told her I'm not excited for anything at all.

*November 7th*
I kind of miss my obsessions and my anxiety. At least I cared about stuff. I was happy and I was sad, now I'm just numb. Now, this journal feels like me trying to care. I am expected to write a deep and meaningful reflection, but I don't have one. I live. I was given a pen. I write stuff. If I don't write stuff, I'll be "non-compliant" and checked in somewhere against my will by my parents.

*November 20th*
They took away any sharp objects. I found one of those short pencils used for filling out forms in the visitor's lounge. It's dull, so they haven't taken it yet. I make circles with my thumb over the small nub of graphite when I hide it in the sleeve of my sweater. The fluorescent lights are blinking a lot. The texture of my blanket is an annoying mix between Velcro and felt. They gave me decaf. Placebo coffee is a bigger lie than my antidepressants.

*November 29th*
I have a roommate. Her name is Judy. She asked me mine. I had trouble hearing the question in real time so I stared at her until she left the room. Then, I remembered what she had said as it echoed in my brain and answered "Hailey" to no one.

*Self-portrait #1 (top), Self-portrait #3 (bottom) by Ace Tilton Ratcliff*

# Community, Identity, and My Gifted Diagnosis

by Lys Morton

*Content note: ableism, exclusion, descriptions of sensory distress/ overload, and brief mention of PTSD, depression, anxiety, and sexual assault*

There's this question I've been asking myself the last few years, as I explore disability, neurodiversity, and the activism wrapped in these communities. Where my role was in it all as I found myself shifting from ally to member of these communities.

This journey started off with me looking for adult voices for the kids I worked with in the private school I volunteered at so often they finally hired me. The staff around me talked routinely about how important role models and representation were for our students. So, I went looking for those role models. And found them I did.

It was jarring, to say the least, as I was faced with these role models telling me that the language we curated at the school would be doing more harm than good. Terms like "child with autism" did more to separate my students from chunks of their identity than to help them feel "more than just a diagnosis." Telling our students that everyone in the class was "friend" wasn't the best way to teach social boundaries. And that we really should be working with stims instead of against them.

In all the information these role models shared with me, I found echoes of my own struggles. And now I'm fighting with imposter syndrome, various levels of internalized ableism, and struggles with a diagnosis that few would consider a hindrance.

My gifted diagnosis has come with a fascinating parade of criticism trailing behind it. It's been 16 years since I received the diagnosis at the ripe old age of nine, and I'm confident saying I've heard just about all the criticisms out there. Contrary to what others might think, my mom did not sit me at the dinner table every night, drilling flash card drills into my head. I do not think that a gifted diagnosis is a classist, racist, ableist term. It's not just some "fancy" version of autism. And no, it's not just a couple of extra points on an IQ test.

People focus on the idea of gifted people being prodigy-level geniuses so there are many facets of the gifted diagnosis that few people discuss. For example, childhood depression or the hypersensitivity that can manifest as sensory processing disorder (SPD). People see "talents" and not the massive asynchronous development that is directly correlated to being gifted. They want to talk about how quickly gifted kids pick up on things, yet they struggle to understand how that ties in with the near manic energy that pours out of the kid.

Thanks in part to this discourse, I was twenty when I finally learned that giftedness was more than high IQ points. I was already on my way to becoming an adult when I realized there was a reason why my fine motor skills matched that of the average seven-year-old. It took until my first year of university to come to grips with the fact that the agitated energy leading to days of sleepless nights was not something I could "grow out of." I was overwhelmed with new information that turned a spotlight onto a part of my identity I'd paid little attention to.

So many things clicked as my understanding went from wondering what the hell was wrong with me to realizing the various aspects that overlapped. It was a fascinating little turmoil to embark on in my first year of university. I finally had answers to the meltdowns, sensory issues, and various quirks as they all became supercharged by the stress of post-secondary.

With knowledge comes more questions, like what could I do about my ever-fluctuating focus which drove me between school work and Wikipedia odysseys of studying the history of scaphism? What about my sensory system that was hypersensitive to lights in my classes, but couldn't remind me to eat for days on end? Was there ever going to be relief from the sudden rushes of emotions that left me either in exhaustive fits of laughter or in bed-ridden throes of depression? How could I manage the leaps and bounds of topical connections my brain made during an average conversation?

At first, I found little community in my gifted diagnosis. I think that internal shame wraps people up so tightly that they can't fathom reaching out to others with the same diagnosis. In my first year of university, I was desperate for some form of community; I was desperate for answers on how I was supposed to live with this odd little diagnosis everyone thought I would "grow out of" by the time I had graduated high school; desperate to know how to make the world feel a little more in sync with me.

I began to dip my toes in Disability groups once again, going back to those role models I'd found for my students the years before. Scouring books, roaming through YouTube, and diving head first into Tumblr. Discovering the hashtag #ActuallyAutistic lead to #Stimtastic lead to #SensoryLife, and I started to find my role models.

Although SPD is a part of a gifted diagnosis, you're never really told outright "you have sensory issues." As I slowly immersed myself into the SPD community, I was incredibly self-conscious of any move I might make that would somehow show I was a fraud. As if the fact that I was a grown adult who still gagged when food touched on his plate, or that I struggled to eat anything outside five specific textures, or that I carried a backpack crammed full of books on the way to class for the deep pressure wasn't enough to really have sensory issues. Regardless, I still wondered if I should just be thankful for my "gift" and if I was just selfishly seeking attention. I still felt like I didn't quite belong.

Slowly, I adopted the language found in the SPD community, and then the neurodivergent community, and then the Disability community. I discovered stimming and suddenly the stressful biting and picking of my skin was no longer "an annoying habit." With that came the knowledge on how to shift a stim from self-harming to healthier stims, like fiddling with a toy. The idea of sensory meltdowns explained my days of breaking down from an onslaught of external stimuli, and I learned how to better regulate my senses to ward off the meltdowns. I no longer told myself I was being lazy when I discovered the concept of brain fog. And then I found spoon theory, sensory diets, self-care, and so on.

I felt like a scavenger, quietly snagging resources only to scurry off back to my dorm room to read through them. I tried out tips and advice from others to see what helped and what hindered, sneakily exploring resources I felt I had no right to access. As my knowledge grew, I began opening up about it, sharing strategies for those who spoke about struggles and had no diagnosis yet.

Over time, I became the sensory guy among my peers. I would arrive to class in sunglasses and with stim toys, notice the signs of sensory overload in my peers, and rant about the fluorescent lights and constant sound of on-campus construction. But when asked what it was that created this need for personal awareness, I clammed up. I balked at the idea of divulging what my diagnosis actually was, yet again struggling with that notion I should be thankful for my "gift" and be flourishing without outside help. I was worried people would see me as encroaching on communities I didn't belong in, taking resources and terms that weren't for me to use. I continued to struggle with these insecurities while trying to find vocabulary and strategies that aided in my day-to-day life.

Then, I found the term that flung my internal identity debate into a whole new light: internalized ableism. I was struggling to claim the identity of Disabled because of a nagging voice in the back of my mind saying, "There's nothing wrong with you, though. You're just gifted." How dare I claim that being gifted was a disability when so many people congratulated me on it. How dare I struggle with this gift.

I am more open to saying I have SPD than I am with saying I'm gifted. I'll most likely divulge that I have PTSD, am a sexual assault survivor, struggle with depression and anxiety, and am a Transgender male before I will consider opening up about being gifted. I've been wrestling with this very piece you're reading since the day I first thought of writing it.

If my giftedness is really a gift, then it's a gift that saddled me with depression and anxiety at age nine. It's a gift that charges my nervous system with an exorbitant amount of information, leading to days where the very thought of trying to change my clothes feels like a physical attack. A gift that has put my schooling in jeopardy because I fixate on the project that won't even be due until next semester instead of on the assignment that was due last week. A gift that puts my health in constant flux as I swing between sleepless nights and days of aggressive physical activity for the sensory input of it all.

But there *is* a gift in finding the language that helps you better understand yourself. In learning the skills others have found before you that help you navigate your world. In finding others who understand just how at odds you can be with a world not designed for you. In being able to see yourself, your struggles, your quirks in others.

There is nothing wrong with being Disabled. There *is* something wrong with shame denying you the community and knowledge you need to survive and thrive.

*And Yet I Shine by Ciro di Ruocco*

# Pill Poppers
by Fira

*Content note: ableism, medication, mention of self-harm, brief mention of gun
(metaphor)*

"The sign of a good doctor should be how many people he gets off
medications, not how many people he puts on medications."

This motivational mess crossed my Facebook feed
the day after I finally convinced my doctor I could not fight my illness
alone.
It was the first day I woke up safe in my own brain
three diagnoses in as many years
and not a single one respected.
I had to fight for every pill that keeps me even keel to this day
lose one and the whole house of cards comes down.

I knew I could not explain this to someone who had never lived
through it
so I tried to be polite in my response:
I told them some people need medication to be safe.
Because it's not polite to tell them of the scars on my skin from
digging up an enemy in my veins,
it's not polite to tell them there is no herbal tea or long walk that will
make me want to live
it's not polite to tell them that at 23 I told my best friend what to put
on my gravestone.

In high school, a girl talked about starting yet another ineffective
therapy so she wouldn't have to be "popping pills."
At every family dinner, I sit through the same well-intentioned aunt
touting the glory of pseudoscience and self-control over "using
drugs."
Talked about with the same less-than, side-eye bullshit
that hurts those of us who found our own help on the street
whether it was to feel something that wasn't pain
or because clinics don't give out scripts to keep you sane

when we're all pill poppers and drug users,
looked down on for how we choose to get by—
What you call us
is how you see us.
Know you can never understand our choices without respecting our
struggles.

We live in a world where excess is strength and mercy is weakness:
Applaud the one who works themself to death,
but do not extend a hand to help them off their knees.
There is only glory in the journey if your pilgrimage is a solo one,
flagellation preferred,
people want to see you bleed
forgetting that some of us are nursing wounds each morning
because we just made it through the darkest night of our lives.
Night
after night
after night.
Keeping the faith that this night will be brighter,
this day will be better,
this life will be worth it.

Next time someone tells me we should be drug-free,
I will remind them
that clean and alive are not always synonyms
We are not asking for a magic bullet,
only for help unloading the gun
when our default state is Russian roulette.
If asking for help is weakness,
then we are all made of glass,
bulletproof glass
we break but don't shatter,
thanking the doctors who knew better
than to shame us off our medications.

# Safe Hands: a poem for autistic youth

by Marrok Zenon Sedgwick

Leaves flutter, beckoning
like butterflies
our hands flap to caress them,
celebrating!
"Safe Hands!" you swat.
Our butterflies slap to our sides,
wet with fear
slip into our pockets
defeated.
What was unsafe?
Was it our joy?

# On Valentine's Day, Let's Recognize Why #AccessIsLove

by Alice Wong

Roses, chocolates, galentines . . . there is a lot of emphasis on love for people in our personal lives this time of year. I could cry into my glass of rosé over the lack of romance in my life but instead, I'm going to send this valentine to the communities I'm a part of and share how their love sustains me.

I spent much of my childhood and young adulthood finding myself and community. I didn't have the words or concepts such as "ableism" or "intersectionality" that helped shape me into who I am today. Disability pride and identity took a long time for me to develop and the process accelerated once I started reaching out to other Disabled people. They didn't have to look exactly like me or become my best friend, but I received a glimmer of recognition, the "Yeah, I got you" understanding of our lived experiences that kept me going.

When I first moved to the San Francisco Bay Area 22 years ago, I felt like a Midwestern suburban mouse arriving at the epicentre of crip culture. Disabled women and Disabled people of colour, in particular, embraced me, sharing their lives, time, and culture with me. My self-education grew as I learned about disability justice and connected with people online beyond the Bay Area bubble.

As I began to embrace and accept myself, I had to acknowledge the messiness, shame, and internalized ableism that will always be a part of me. It is thanks to the love and generosity of Disabled people that I have opened up to new ways of being, thinking, and moving in the world. Individual acts of love and kindness became part of a larger collective force holding everyone together with bonds of interdependence.

Every community, big or small, has conflict, drama, and a whole lot of dysfunction. Every community also has a reservoir of intergenerational wisdom, energy, and love that has the power to build, create, and mobilize for change. As a member of multiple communities, I love them all because they anchor me while providing freedom to splash around with joy unapologetically, grow, and carve out new spaces in collaboration with others.

Last fall, after years of friendship, I got to spend time in person with two friends of mine, Mia Mingus and Sandy Ho. We talked about Mia's keynote address at the 2018 Disability Intersectionality Summit (an event led and organized by Sandy) called "Disability Justice is Simply Another Term for Love." This quote from Mia resonated with me deeply:

> "I would argue that 'disability justice' is simply another term for love. And so is 'solidarity,' 'access,' and 'access intimacy.' I would argue that our work for liberation is simply a practice of love—one of the deepest and most profound there is. And the creation of this space is an act of love."

Magic happens when you get brilliant Disabled people together. During our conversation about how we can advance these ideas in a creative and fun way, a new project was born: #AccessIsLove. Created by Mia, Sandy, and myself, we launched a campaign with the following goals:
- Expand the idea of access beyond compliance and the disability rights framework
- Encourage people to incorporate accessibility in their everyday practices and lives
- Show solidarity and give support to activists across movements outside and within the Disability community

We created a list of resources on accessibility and disability justice and ten steps people can take to start thinking and acting intentionally about access. We also designed some merchandise to raise money for a different advocacy group every two months to give material support and show solidarity. For example, during February and March 2019, all proceeds from our online store went to the House of GG, the first national retreat site, educational and historical centre solely dedicated to Transgender and gender nonconforming people in the US.

With all of this in mind, on this Valentine's Day I invite you to think about these questions:
- Who do you love? Who are your people?
- How do you show love for your communities?

- What does it mean to show up for others?
- In what ways is access, solidarity, and disability justice a form of love?

Who we love and how we love is inherently political. We declare our kinship through our actions and words in both explicit and subtle ways. It's not easy or simple, but I hope everyone will find their people and ways to express love for their communities each and every day.

*In this photo: Alice Wong (centre), Mia Mingus (left), and Sandy Ho (right) at the 2018 Disability Intersectionality Summit.*

# River Fatigue

by Niamh Timmons

*Content note: fatigue flare*

For once I have enough energy to go hike
so let's walk down a river trail
When we reach a clearing along the river,
I'll tell you I need to rest
"It's beautiful here,"
you nod your head
"I was talking about you,"
you lean toward me to kiss me
I lose my balance as your lips press against me
I cling to you
"Are you okay?" you ask
I nod and press against you more but you keep your balance
After a few minutes I'm out of breath and need to stop
I didn't mean to give you what little energy I had left
I hobble back on the trail with you
telling you to take me back home with you

Next season, when I tell you about my muscles aching,
I'll ask you to gently undress me
kiss me where the muscles tense
Don't be alarmed when the first sprouts emerge
and rest with me while I germinate.

*From Bed by Jessi Eoin*

*Disability: Asthma, dysautonomia, myalgic encephalomyelitis*

*Gender: Nonbinary woman*

*Pronouns: She/her and they/them*

*Sexuality: Pansexual*

*Romantic attraction: Biromantic*

# Spoons
by Nina Fosati

*Content note: seizure, hospitalization, mention of* death

We spoon together, he and I. It's how we fall asleep each night;
cradled together. He massages my aching muscles; his warm hands
soothe me. This end-of-day ritual is sacred to me now and I can't
fall asleep without it. Usually he falls asleep first. His breathing slows
and his hands start to twitch as his body discharges the day's excess
energy. I cherish these moments because I know they are a gift. One I
almost never knew.

I lay prone on the bathroom floor. My body wheezed as I struggled
for air. Three months of inactivity after surgery for a bruised spinal
cord had led to the development of pulmonary embolisms. When
the paramedics flipped me over, a burning spotlight ringed with
static filled my eyes and another seizure took hold. They sedated me,
strapped me to a board for the halting, rocking ride down the stairs
to the first floor, then outside and down the porch steps. I lay on a
gurney next to the ambulance, snow almost reaching my fingertips. It
was the coldest day of the New Year, a meager -11° Celsius.

"Please don't take me to the hospital," I mumbled. Then, as we
rolled away, "Is the siren on? I can barely hear it."

After several tests, the doctors told me I had developed seizures
because my blood oxygen level had fallen too low. It was serious.
There were dozens of blood clots littering both lungs and pulmonary
arteries. I was lucky to be alive. The clots could travel to my brain
and cause a stroke or lodge in the arteries of my heart and stop
its beating. They were fighting the complications with all the logic,
chemicals, and tests available but my situation was dangerous. Was
my end-of-life paperwork in order?

People streamed in and out of my hospital room in a confusing
succession of poke and prod, test and question. I tried to be a
patient patient, but I had a hard go of it. I got sick of being sick, sick
of smelling and tasting like chemicals, sick of my roommate Mother
Merris, sick of the hundreds of little humiliations. On the fourth day I
decided to tell people who walked in, no matter their status or role,
"I want to go home." I hoped that if I said it enough times, eventually

someone would release me.

Two days later, I sat in my reclining chair with a cotton blanket wrapped around my shoulders, another draped over my naked legs, arguing with the chilly air leaching through the windows. Noting my agitation, a nurse had pulled the privacy curtain around my half of the room and closed the blinds, leaving me in a semi-private anti-stimulation chamber. This did little to help my distress. I could still hear the bonging of monitor alarms up and down the floor, conversations in the corridor, and an impersonal female voice directing nurses and aides to assist patients via the PA system. The announcements were one of the grand indignities of being in the hospital. After a while you learned to decode them, and they usually boiled down to excretions. If someone called for help—needed a bedpan, a walk to the toilet, or a diaper change—their demand was announced to the floor.

My roommate was an elderly black woman. Mother Merris had a large family and a church connection. The difference in our level of support depressed me. I was disappointed there were few phone calls and no cards or flowers to surprise or distract me. Careful about sharing medical information, my husband hadn't told our friends the gravity of my situation. Upon hearing someone has a blood clot, people often think, "Nana had one in her leg. It was no big deal."

The unintentional consequence of his protecting my privacy left me feeling abandoned and friendless. My husband would sneak into my room for a few minutes before work and come back for an hour or so after dinner, but I was left largely on my own to endure the long days and nights.

I might have felt less forsaken if my roommate's multiple visitors hadn't started arriving at 11a.m. and stayed until visiting hours ended at nine p.m. They brought her presents and food every day. Hearing the crinkle of her unwrapping hard candies and chocolates irritated me.

Sitting in my chilly recliner, I could hear the babble of people helping my roommate prepare to leave for physical rehabilitation. I had to fight my gloominess, so I put on my headphones and thumbed on my favorite music. I was going to sing along. Loudly. I needed comfort and I didn't care who heard. So what if they stared at the beige curtain separating us, their heads shaking or their shoulders twitching with suppressed laughter?

I warbled along to my favorite tunes. Bruce Springsteen's "For You" came on. I had focused on this song for months prior to my hospital stay. It was part of an ongoing reassessment of my life, a reflection on choices made, paths taken and not. Lyrics that had no significance previously plunged into my mood and grabbed my emotions. With my nose clogged and eyes brimming over, I could barely breathe through the sadness, yet I continued to sing.

The song had transformed. Part of it was about an old decision, a man denied and turned away. Part of it was about my life now. References to the ambulance ride, oxygen masks, compromised lungs and the heart being the key wrecked me. This song was about the fact that I almost died.

I had wasted decades drifting away from my husband. Recently, we had fought our way back to each other. After finding trust and love again, I'd almost left him—albeit unintentionally, but still. I thought I had years left to carefully, gently rebuild, and it could have crashed down on that one day. I gulped and sobbed, but my tears helped wash away the fear of the past week. They helped revive my spirit, and I found the courage to face the weary days of rehab ahead, when I would relearn how to stand and walk again.

Someone once said, "Every good marriage ends in tragedy." The line has stuck with me. Near the end of a life together, it's usually the woman who is left to live her last decades alone without physical comfort and companionship.

My husband and I have a secret understanding. I will die first. I will leave him alone and for that, I weep—for the sorrow, pain, and loneliness my passing will one day cause him. Six months before my hospital stay, I had been on the brink of walking out on him. If we hadn't fought to reconnect, he would have lost a housemate, a friend, a companion instead of losing his best friend, his lover, his wife. Now, we spoon together, he and I. It's how we fall asleep each night; cradled together.

# Just Like You
by Isabella J. Mansfield

*Content notes: ableism, inspiration porn, inaccessibility*

On Sunday, I go to the farmer's market where I am called "little lady" despite being a 37-year-old woman.

On Monday, I go to the grocery store, where I am stopped by no less than three people who tell me I am "so brave."

On Tuesday, at dinner, they talk to my husband instead of me and tell him what a good man he is for marrying me.

On Wednesday, I go to the gym and boys offer to help me with the weights. What exactly do they think I am doing there?

On Thursday, I am inspirational because I pumped my own gas.

On Friday, I almost miss the movie while I wait to pee because someone is using the only accessible toilet as a phone booth.

On Saturday, there is no ramp into the bar, the bartender doesn't see me, the only tables are high tops, and four drunk guys are staring down my shirt from their bar stool perches.

On Sunday, they tell me they know just what it's like because one time they spent a whole month in a wheelchair after breaking a leg at camp.

On Monday, I don't need your help loading my groceries into my car, thank you. No, really. NO, REALLY. No! Okay, fine.

On Tuesday, a mother at the park tells her children not to stare at me or ask questions because it's rude.

On Wednesday, they act surprised when I tell them I have a child and then ask personal questions about the delivery, pregnancy, and even the act of conception.

On Thursday, I have to try on those clothes at home and hope they fit because the accessible fitting room is *used for storage, sorry! Oh, no, we don't accept returns either.*

On Friday, I ask three drunk strangers to watch my drink, my purse, and my chair so I can use the bar bathroom that isn't accessible at all and is so dirty and I have to touch every surface just to stop from falling.

On Saturday, I watch my son from the playground bench. I'm tired so it's fine, but I couldn't get through the sandbox or woodchips if I wanted to.

On Sunday, I'm quoted in an article about poetry but instead of using my quotes about poetry, they focus on my disability and I'm misquoted about "how nice it is to feel included."

On Monday, I argue with the manager at the grocery store for the fourth time in a month for blocking the sidewalk with palettes of rock salt.

On Tuesday, they plow snow over the ramps and into accessible parking stalls.

On Wednesday, I recall being separated from my classmates on field trips due to inaccessible transportation and thoughtless administrators.

On Thursday, I remember the ex-boyfriend who threw my chair across the garage because *he* was the frustrated one.

On Friday, they told me they wouldn't be able to get out of bed or leave the house, if they were me.

On Saturday, I stay home, not because I am homebound, wheelchair-bound or bound by any of your expectations of Disability.

On Sunday, I go to the farmer's market.

On Monday, I go to the grocery store.

On Tuesday, I go out with my husband.

On Wednesday, I go to the gym.

On Thursday, I go out with my family.

On Friday, I go to the playground with my son.

On Saturday, I go out with my friends.

Just like you.

*The Future is Accessible by Eryn Goodman*

# When The Rainbow is All You Have, It Has to Be Enuf

by K. Bron Johnson

*Content note: mention of suicide, ableist slurs, profanity*

*"this is for colored girls who have considered suicide / but are movin to the ends of their own rainbows."*
>  -Ntozake Shange in *For Colored Girls Who Have Considered Suicide/When the Rainbow is Enuf*

When my best friend from childhood was preparing to marry her husband who is in the army, she knew she would have to follow him across the country to live wherever they were stationed. Soon after they married, she learned she would be moving from her hometown of Montreal to a base across the country. She knew nothing about the town they were moving to and didn't know anyone who lived there, other than her husband. I remember telling her: "He has to be enuf."

In other words, when missing the familiar foods, sights, and faces of home, he will have to be enough to make up for everything else. If he is all she has, he has to be everything. Not forever, hopefully, but until she could make new friends and experiences and memories. That one thing she was holding onto had to be everything and enough.

It was rough at first. Struggling to fit in, she found she hated their new town and became depressed. However, she got a job and made friends, slowly. She accepted she would be there for a while and made the most of it. The place she was initially uncertain about became a place she didn't want to leave. In the end, she bore her two children there. As if by magic, it all became enuf for her.

Her story is important to me because I liken her move across the country to my diagnosis journey. Before I was diagnosed with autism, I knew there was something different about me, but I didn't know why I was different. Without a reason to attribute my struggles to, the only conclusion I could come to was that I was broken. Somehow I had failed as a human. No matter how hard I tried, everyone was able to notice I was different. My parents never missed an opportunity to tell me the way I did things was "illogical" or "weird" and my way of thinking simply flawed, while simultaneously marvelling at my ability to excel at school or dance. Unable to forge friendships that lasted with most kids without getting bullied, I sought out the company of what my mother called "the underdogs"—the Disabled kids, the fat kids, the troubled kids, the poor kids, the ones no one else wanted to be friends with.

I hated myself. I could not see my value. Despite my good marks in school and my behaviour that made teachers say things like, "she's so quiet. A model student! Never gets into trouble. Never complains," I had no self-esteem. I was uncomfortable in my school uniform and in my own skin. I thought I was broken. My parents called me "stupid" and "idiot" on a regular basis. I wanted to die. I thought nobody cared or wanted to associate with someone as "broken" as me.

When I think of the times in my life I contemplated suicide, I can't for the life of me remember what it was that really kept me going, kept me here. What was my "enuf?" I remember sometimes just hoping to make it to 18 years old. That was the magical age I needed to get to in order to move out and move on. Or, maybe I thought I would be "normal" then.

Regardless, I'm glad I came out the other side because, over time, I went from wondering why I was "broken" and "stupid" and "incapable of ever amounting to anything," to being able to appreciate my brain for all it is, the good with the bad.

I'm hyperlexic, which means I had the precocious ability to read above my age level as a child. As an adult, I benefit from it by being able to scan a text very quickly and understand what is in the text. Because of that and my photographic memory, I learn extremely quickly, am able to memorize facts, and have a fascination with languages. I can scan a page of text and spot grammatical errors with laser-like focus and I will find bugs in code without understanding programming language (because bugs don't fit the pattern or syntax), but I can't tie my shoes properly. I can't follow a conversation if more than two people are talking. My executive functioning skills are shit. I have the worst time trying to figure out if people are lying to me. I struggle with sensory overload and anxiety.

This is just the brain I've been given. This is all I have and it's as if I've been dropped in the middle of nowhere with just this brain of mine. In the end, if I didn't want to suffer, I had to accept it and it had to be enough. Not perfect, but enuf. So, what changed?

Six months after my best friend gave birth to her first child, I had a son. He was a little male version of me. He was quirky and sensitive and became overloaded with the world easily. He ate very limited foods and was nonverbal. He hummed, and flapped, and stared at the spinning wheels of his toy cars and trains for what seemed like hours. I strangely related to him and how he behaved. Shortly after his neurodiversity diagnosis, something clicked and I visited a psychologist to tell me if I had a neurodiverse brain as well. Finally, it all made sense. I wasn't broken! I was not a failed human! Instead, I had just been living in a new town, not realizing I was speaking the language but it wasn't my native tongue. With this new information, I was able to start the journey into knowing who I was. I was able to reach a place of acceptance. And where did that acceptance come from? Understanding and empathy.

Neurodiversity is depicted by an icon that's a rainbow-coloured infinity loop. Since autism is a spectrum disorder—meaning there are a range of conditions under the umbrella of autism spectrum disorder—I like to say I have a rainbow brain since a rainbow spans all colours. When you look at me quickly, you might not realize I have a rainbow brain unless you know what you are looking for. Over time, I have adapted to the language and ways of the world around me. There are parts of the spectrum that affect me that you can't see, but get to know me over time and my true colours start to show: my tics (the way I crack my neck) and my stims (the way I fiddle with my hands, bite my nails, rub my eyes, and pull my eyelashes). Different colours of the spectrum shine brighter, but all of them together make up my rainbow brain.

I have needed to cultivate understanding and empathy for myself because until I understood myself, my complete autistic self in all my glory, I could not accept myself or my rainbow brain. I needed to learn how to have the grace with myself that I gave to others, fully accepting others how they are. In order to find the treasure at the end of my own rainbow, I needed to learn to have empathy for myself, for my rainbow brain and all its failings and strengths.

I'd love to say that I did it all by myself, that I didn't need a psychologist to validate me and tell me who I was and what type of brain I had, but diagnosis was a gift I gave myself.

Like my friend with her move, once I understood who I was and accepted myself for who I was, I was able to make friends and find my people. I could throw out the old stuff I didn't need and choose to redecorate my world with things that bring me happiness, peace, and comfort. Now that I've gone to the end of my rainbow, I can't imagine ever leaving. It's enuf for this coloured girl.

It's enuf.

It's enuf.

I'm enuf.

# Falling Masonry
by Jan Steckel

Word salad for breakfast again as pain meds duke it out with
Darjeeling.
     If I beat up the berries in my oatmeal,
will I get black and blueberries?
        If I put an orange in my porringer,
    will it make my porridge oranger?

I dressed in corporate style for the luncheon
to show I recognize social signals.

     If I had to re-dress in my red dress,
          I would have no redress.
       When I get this feeling,
        I need textual healing.

          When I mean to say "Ovid's Metamorphoses"
             it comes out "Ovid's Metastases."

        I have to plaster my place in Post-its
          to remember my daily to-dos.

         I spend more time writing it
           down than actually doing it.

       The neurologist sent me to a sleep lab,
         where I rose gasping out of the
           deep four times an hour.

     Told me I have sleep apnea,
       need a CPAP machine.

   So, I strap myself into fighter-pilot headgear
     to fly through dreams every night.

In my sleep, I've tied the plastic tubing;
I breathe through a knot.

Every time I mean one thing but say another,
I learn more about my brain's architecture
as it falls down around me.
Shall I clean up the mess myself?
I'm having too much fun.
Straw-hatted, to the Ladies' Luncheon, I breeze.
Someone else will sweep up the rubble when I go.

*Cripple Punk Portrait #17 by Michaela Oteri*

# Valuing Activism of All Kinds

by Alice Wong

Recently, Disabled activists from ADAPT protested in Washington, DC as the House debated the American Health Care Act (AHCA). Fifty-four badass Disabled people put their bodies on the line, chanting and drawing media attention on what is at stake if the AHCA passes. They were arrested inside the Capitol Rotunda for obstructing passage in a public building. They made, in the words of Representative John Lewis, good trouble.

I felt immense pride seeing Disabled people practice civil disobedience and defend the right of all people to basic health coverage. In the back of my mind, I also felt a twinge of envy. I miss the camaraderie of being in a large group of Disabled people fighting the system. It was an immature case of Activism FOMO (fear of missing out).

As I questioned my feelings, I realized I still wrestle with mainstream notions of what it means to be an "activist" and the centreing of non-Disabled constructs of what it means to "show up" in rallies, town halls, marches, or protests. Maybe it's because I'm getting older, but I do prefer to stay home—I don't need to worry about weather, transportation, attendants' schedules, or the lack of accessible bathrooms in public spaces. This is why I am grateful for the privilege of having a fast broadband connection, laptop, and love of social media. While it can feel lonely organizing from home, I have to remind myself that the activism I am involved with now is both complementary to and is as legitimate as other traditional forms. Different modes, same goals.

For instance, last year Gregg Beratan, Andrew Pulrang, and I created #CripTheVote, an online movement encouraging the political participation of people with disabilities. The three of us use Twitter to keep the movement going and with our hashtag we've seen the Disability community come together in powerful ways. Last year, Rooted in Rights gathered #CripTheVote stories from Disability activists around the country.

#CripTheVote recently hosted a chat on the American Health Care Act and its impact on disabled people. Here's a brief snapshot of the main themes from the online discussion:

Healthcare is more than just medical services for people with disabilities.

Julia Bascom
@JustStimming

Medicaid provides most home & community-based services (HCBS). #savemedicaid #CripTheVote

♡ 7  3:10 PM - Mar 21, 2017  ⓘ

See Julia Bascom's other Tweets  >

Block grants and other efforts to cut Medicaid will have disastrous repercussions for Disabled people.

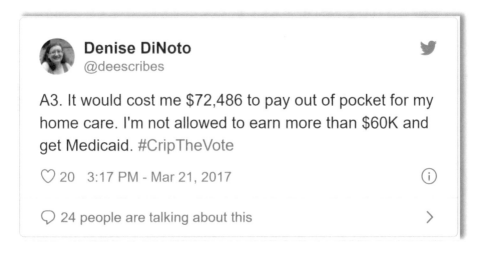

Denise DiNoto
@deescribes

A3. It would cost me $72,486 to pay out of pocket for my home care. I'm not allowed to earn more than $60K and get Medicaid. #CripTheVote

♡ 20  3:17 PM - Mar 21, 2017  ⓘ

⤵ 24 people are talking about this  >

Healthcare is a right, not a luxury.

 **Alice Wong** @DisVisibility · Mar 21, 2017
Q4: What are some core provisions and services disabled people should require from any healthcare bill? #CripTheVote

 **Alexander Calhoun**
@AlexCalhoun23

A4: The right to stay at home, access to physical and mental health services, care regardless of condition. #CripTheVote

♡ 5   3:30 PM - Mar 21, 2017

Attempts to repeal the Affordable Care Act will unravel the decades of activism by the Disability community.

 **Lindsay Baran**
@lindsay_baran

A5 Huge concern is per capita caps & block grants. Cuts to Medicaid mean disabled ppl will be forced into institutions and die. #CripTheVote

♡ 102   3:29 PM - Mar 21, 2017   ⓘ

💬 68 people are talking about this

People with disabilities are scared, for many good reasons.

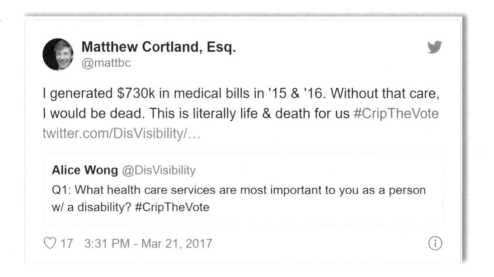

Participants gave real-life examples of the importance of healthcare on their lives, ideas for improving policies and services for people with disabilities, and actions people can take to become politically engaged.

Looking ahead, I know that activism in all of its forms (e.g., letter writing, making phone calls, protesting, Twitter chats, storytelling) will be needed in order to mobilize and organize a coalition of diverse communities with common political goals and that each kind of activism has a unique purpose and power.

The next time I develop symptoms of Activism FOMO, I'm going to tell myself: "Do what you can, however you can. All efforts are valuable. And get over yourself!"

# Companions

by Nina Fosati

*Content note: physical rehabilitation (aqua therapy), descriptions of physical pain*

I stand at the edge of the pool looking down at the clear, blue water. Five steps. That's all it will take. Five steps and the water will help me feel better. Aqua therapy pools are rare in Western New York. With a treadmill submerged in one corner, this one is perhaps the rarest of all. My son and I have searched for weeks for a pool I felt safe entering. We decided this one in Orchard Park suits me best.

Handrails line both sides of the staircase, each a comfortable distance apart. Black anti-slip tape is wrapped at intervals down their length. Gripping both, I carefully lower my left foot onto the submerged first step. I cannot sense temperature in my feet and the soothing warmth of the water barely registers. My right foot follows the left, marking the beginning of my careful descent into the pool. I have done this two times a week for the past six months.

I pause on the third step where the water is up to my thighs. On the fourth step, the heaviness lightens. I hop off the last step and the heated water welcomes me, enfolds my body. I live for the moment when the weight lifts off my joints, and magically, my companion and I separate. I soak in the welcome sensation; take a moment to savour the feeling. No pain.

Normally, there are others in the pool and the loneliness of being Disabled leads to a shared camaraderie. We tell each other about our injuries, our operations, how we have failed to heal or re-injured ourselves. We open up to each other about our grievances, our trials. We share more quickly and openly than strangers usually do because our time together is limited. We share because we live with pain. The abled-bodied can't understand.

Our physicians have prescribed this therapy because our bodies are beyond the normal bounds of physical rehabilitation. Our jagged bones scrape and grind against each other. Our backs send searing pain with each movement. We try not to cry out, but the pain escapes as moans, sudden inhalations, searing hisses. We make the sounds people expect of the elderly. We move slowly, robotically, while intently focusing on each step. We gently test before each change of position.

I straddle the treadmill, make certain my feet are off the belt, then press the start button and adjust the speed to the slowest setting. Taking my hands off the railings, I begin my Zombie-like walk. I tilt and stutter, making my jolting, flat-footed way down an imaginary path.

One woman shares the pool with me today. She's doing her exercises in the shallow end. We have never met, but I like her spirit. Over my shoulder, I tell her about an old friend from high school who has recently reconnected with me. I am tender-hearted about the time we shared. Perhaps it is just sentimentality, but I am looking forward to renewing our bond. I'm wondering if it is possible to go back to being as close as we once were.

"I don't know why I'm telling you this," I smile.

"Because you need to," she replies.

I think she is right.

She takes a breath. "I'm a loner," she says. "I never made many friends, but now that I'm 65, I'm wondering if I should have tried harder. It's difficult to make friends when you're older."

I know what she means. I can see she is on the brink of asking if I'd like to go out for coffee, to take a stab at being more than companions, but we are both in the pool. We will share this half hour, then separate.

I think about my last therapist, Maria, as I'm changing in the locker room. She'd known me at my worst. Back in the days when my body reacted like a startled rabbit trying to dart away from everything. I'd told her that when I drove, every slowdown and flash made my heart race, my breathing quicken, and my calm break away. We met weekly for over a year, then it was time for her to retire. She knew so many intimate details about me and I knew almost nothing about her. I silently longed for a more equitable relationship.

I regarded her from my chair on one side of her cluttered office. I began to talk about the time after she retired when we could be friends. Misinterpreting my eagerness, panic slammed against her eyes, her backpedaling began. Her time would be limited because of her mother's situation. Okay, sure, but I knew it was an excuse nonetheless; I'd overstepped an invisible boundary. Her need did not match mine. After her retirement, I didn't try to reach her for three months. I let inertia run and the time without contact extended to six. Long enough that thoughts of inviting her out to lunch dissipated. On occasion, in the afterglow of a pool session, I half hope she will call or text, having sensed, somehow, that we are now equals, capable of long lunches, laughs, true sharing.

I hoist my bag, packed with my wet swimsuit and towel, before leaving the pool. My dry underwear and summer dress are on. I gently close the metal door of my locker, return the padlock to the front desk, and head for my car. My time in the pool is over. I will return alone in three days.

*Love Etched In by Jessi Eoin*

*Disability: Coronary artery disease with heart transplant*
*Gender: Cisgender woman*

*Pronouns: She/her*
*Sexuality: Pansexual*
*Romantic attraction: Panromantic*

# Horizontal Poet

by Jan Steckel

*Content note: ableist euphemism, descriptions of sex*

"You can't put your mat there," said the nice lady.
"That's for handicapped people."
But I'd been promised I could lie down
when I agreed to read.
"How about there?" I asked.
"Oh no, not there.
We're filming. You'd be in the picture."
"God forbid," I muttered, grinning evilly,
"a disabled person should appear in any pictures."
"Well certainly not lying down.
Not lying down *in public*."

The way she said it, you'd think
I'd asked to have sex in the front of the theatre
all through the reading, my legs in the air,
(my favorite position)
the persistent *thump, thump, thump*
of my pumping and humping
rattling floorboards and shaking the camera,
my caterwauling cries obliterating other poets' readings,
my juices a river flooding the floor and soaking the audience's shoes.

I'll lie down on my job, nice lady.
I'll do it on the hand-hooked Turkish rug
at the invitation-only living-room poetry salon.
I'll do it on the independent bookstore's hardwood.
I'll get Berber carpet burns in the library lecture room.
I'll make listeners hear the person next to them breathe,
make your husband undo his top button and loosen his tie.
I'll make you, sitting properly in your chair,
begin to squirm, then writhe and gasp.
I'll wave my round heels
right in front of your camera,
and I'll *always* be in the picture.

# Ms. Bryant is Dangerously Delusional
by Cathy Bryant

*Content note: ableism, accusations of faking disability, fat phobia*

Note: All these statements about me and my partner, Keir, were said or written by our previous landlords. We were fine tenants but, for reasons unknown to us, they bullied me continually. We sued them and they settled out of court. I believe that they thought my disability meant I was weak and therefore an easy target. They were wrong.

They keep the curtains closed.
Catherine Bryant was (or was feigning to be) asleep.
The plumber will say of the claimant's partner, "He wouldn't let me go upstairs to check the radiators." Other people have found Keir Thomas to be brusque or even threatening.
We were escorted by Keir Thomas and a "friend" who, weighing between 18-20 stone,
was clearly intended to be intimidatory.
They always keep the curtains closed.
You seldom see
the curtains open.
Therefore, I was justifiably angry.
I have had to give the claimant a wide berth, as her inventive malice and the belligerence of her partner causes me to feel nauseated.
The claim is fabricated. The claimant is irrational, vindictive and dangerously delusional. If she can write a letter, then she's not that disabled.
She has taken every opportunity to pursue me with an excess of vindictive communications. She used falsehood in an attempt to justify all the fabrications and exaggerations with which she embellishes her accusations. After all, she does claim to be a "creative writer."
In spite of all her disabilities she was able to visit Heptonstall graveyard—to visit a grave. I believe she is falsely claiming benefits. She is pulling the wool over the taxpayers' eyes.
These videos show her speaking readily and adjusting her clothing

whilst holding a glass. She was apparently well enough to judge a poetry competition.

We do not dispute that Ms. Bryant is disabled. She has made an occupation of tailoring disability to her advantage. I am probably not her first, nor her last victim.

She keeps the curtains closed.

# Night Terrors

by Lara Ameen

*Content note: blood, kidnapping, physical and verbal violence, night terror*

Slowly drifting toward consciousness, my eyes open as I take in my surroundings. A sliver of light streams in through a window at the far end of the room and the iron-rich stench of blood assaults my senses. Flipped on its side, my manual wheelchair remains silhouetted between pale light and murky darkness in the far corner of the room. I look down to see dark red stains clashing against my neatly-pressed white shirt. A drop of blood drips from my nose onto the bloodied fabric.

   Looking up again, my head spins as dizziness clouds my vision. I close my eyes briefly, a respite from the blur of images around me. I open my eyes once more and try to move, but my hands are tied to a wooden post behind my back and my legs are sprawled out in front of me. I am a maze of paralyzed limbs. I can't move and I begin to panic, heartbeat accelerating so fast I can almost hear its thundering *thump, thump, thump* inside my ears. The distant echo of footsteps looms closer, the discordant rhythm of heavy boots hitting cement terrifies me. *Where am I? What's going on?* I wonder to myself.

   A shadowy figure, tall and indistinguishable, enters my line of vision until he steps into the tiny pool of light and turns to look at me. A crooked smile forms on his lips as he leans toward me and though I can't see him well, I can smell the stench of tobacco on his breath. I'm tempted to spit in his face, but he pulls back before I can.

   "It's good to know you're awake, detective. Or should I just call you Lexie?" He studies me with intrigue, desire.

   "Go to hell," I retort.

   "Now, now, sweetheart. We've known each other for how many years?" He chuckles, running a hand through his messy dark hair. "What would your partner think if she found your beautiful, lifeless body here, hmm?"

   "Faber," I grind his name between my clenched teeth. "What do you want? Where did you take me? Where are we?"

   "So many questions," he chides. "Your sister asked a lot of

questions right before I killed her. Had that same horrified look in her eyes until I—"

"Don't you dare bring my younger sister into this!" My throat feels raw and parched when I scream.

"She was pretty," he continues. His tone sends shivers up my spine and goosebumps down my exposed arms. "But you, Lexie, are something else entirely. You are . . . " he pauses, leaning closer to study my features. "A vision. One of a kind."

I do the only thing I can: spit in his face with every ounce of strength I have left. He immediately slaps me across the face with brute force and another scream escapes my lips. I feel my cheek begin to swell and bruise. His laughter reverberates all around me, echoing as if in surround sound that will swallow me alive, swallow me whole.

"Lexie, wake up!"

Another familiar voice enters my consciousness as I come to, bolting upright as my eyes dart around my bedroom. On edge and alert, my heart pounds inside my chest. I see my girlfriend, Heather, sitting beside me, concern in her gentle blue eyes.

"It's okay, Lexie," Heather says to me. She looks at me with concern as she tries to get me to focus. Her eyes meet mine as her hands cup my cheeks. "You're okay," she continues. "You're safe."

She wraps her arms around me and I sob as I lean into her embrace. She presses a gentle kiss into my hair as I attempt to breathe deeply, my body shaking from terror. Heather's presence is warm, comforting, immediate.

After what seems like an interminable stretch of time, I move back as my body relaxes a little. Heather wipes fallen tears from my cheeks.

"You dreamt about Faber again, didn't you?" she asks.

I clench the bed sheets and nod.

"I think my dreams are getting worse," I tell her once I'm able to find my voice. "I can't—I can't keep doing this. I need to find him. I can't afford to fail again."

Heather nods and pulls down the sleeves of her sweater.

"How many more people is he going to kill until he finally kills me, too?" I continue. "He's proven his point. Loud and clear!"

Heather sighs as she shivers. She glances at bright red numbers on the digital alarm clock reading three a.m.

"Lexie, you don't have to get up for another two hours. Maybe you should try and rest a bit more."

"I need to get ready for work," I say, tugging at the covers and scooting toward the side of the bed. My legs dangle precariously over the edge.

Heather watches me. I resist the urge to look back, reassure her, kiss her. The nightmare has my mind set on overdrive, and I have a crystal-clear focus. I know what needs to be done and I want it done now.

I transfer into my wheelchair and steal a glance at her before moving away. She stays silent as I maneuver toward the bathroom, grabbing a fluffy white towel on my way in. I can feel the strain of her worried gaze, begging me to come back and begging me to stay.

As I roll into the bathroom, I can't shake the thought that someone is watching me. Though I can't see anything through the bathroom window, an unsettling sensation crawls across my skin, night terrors coming alive.

*Cripple Punk Portrait #28 by Michaela Oteri*

# Aisle Nine: Bottled Water, Juice, Clearance, Bible Verses,Unwanted Attention
by Isabella J. Mansfield

*Content note: unsolicited praying, church/religion, brief mention of food*

a man prayed over me in the clearance aisle
of my neighbourhood grocery store,
for my healing, for the health of my "broken" body.
called me "sister"
said "it isn't enough to just say the words,
you have to give them power, you have to feel it."

I couldn't tell him
people have laid their hands
on me in every grocery store
from here to Arizona,
for the last twenty-five years
and all it's ever done is make me late
or melt the ice cream in my bag.

I couldn't tell him
that a miracle would be nice
but I'm not holding my breath
on the thoughts and the prayers,
for the day he'll see me turn cartwheels
down that very aisle.

I couldn't tell him
I was in a crisis of faith
unrelated to my "condition,"
how I feel empty

inside a crowded church
and I'm not bothered by this.

because I can't miss something
if I'm not really sure
it was ever there.

# Social Cues Missed

by Kimberley Hunter

*Content note: ableism*

When I'm in a room full of people,
autism leaves me feeling out of place
like a giraffe in a crowd of Oompa Loompas.
That feeling follows me
everywhere, like a private eye.

A social cue will fly over my head
and land somewhere on the carpet behind me.
I heard them land and know where they are,
but if I go to get them, they are already gone,
evaporated. I wouldn't be able to read them anyway;
those things are written
in a language I don't know.
All I do know about the
language is that it's subtle.
A wink could mean

- encouragement
- a hint at conspiracy

A smile can mean:

- happiness
- facetiousness
- sadness
- stress

Smiling can also mean anger.
And then, there's frowning.
Frowning means:

- anger
- concentration
- a person is sizing another person up
  like the way two members of opposing teams might do
  if they meet each other before a match
- boredom

- maybe apathy
- uncertainty
- horror.

Facial expressions have many meanings;
but I can only interpret some of them
and that isn't nearly enough.

I've had people tell me things like "if you just . . ."
- smiled
- expressed concern.

All of this because of that feeling,
it follows me.

# Create it Away

by Katie Danis

*Content note: descriptions of tics, mention of Catholicism and spirits, food*

I was naked the first time I got my leg stuck in a broken drainpipe. As my preschool teacher dismantled the pipe to free my entrapped and freshly-nude limb, a new crease crept from her cheek to her chin. She was 25 years old and had eight wrinkles; when school began she had zero. In my defense, I held direct responsibility for only seven, and I contest the validity of evidence that charged me with three.

When my parents regaled Dr. McGoogan with my laundry list of strange behaviours,[1] he smiled rows of perfect teeth like books facing the wrong way on a shelf. He handed us glossy white pages that tumbled open to words like "creative" and "neurodivergent" and "comorbidity"—nice words with nice "t"s to turn over and over on your tongue. As I sat on my hands and swung my legs, my eyes wandered over the upside-down scrawl in his notes. *Diagnosis: Tourette Syndrome.*

Tourette Syndrome (also known as Tourette's or TS) is a neurological condition which the National Institute of Neurological Disorders and Stroke (NINDS) defines as being "characterized by repetitive, stereotyped, involuntary movements and vocalizations called tics." TS involves at least one vocal tic. It is hereditary and comorbid with OCD and ADHD. If you have all three diagnoses, congratulations! You win a can of Campbell's Neuropsychological Alphabet Soup. NINDS estimates that 200,000 Americans live with a severe form of TS. The condition is named for neurologist Dr. Georges Gilles de la Tourette, who discovered it in 1885. But I didn't learn any of this until later.

---

1 Including but not limited to banging my head on the floor for hours without cause, hunching over like Quasimodo and clawing out my eyebrows, randomly shrieking as if imitating a stoned screech owl's mating call (and doing a bang-up job, if you ask me), compulsively inhaling underwater, touching my palm to the pavement in the middle of a busy street, and furiously flapping my arms like a 40-pound brunette penguin poised to storm a fishery. You know, normal kid stuff.

For years, I knew Tourette's as my built-in brain gremlin, the voice that commanded me to bang my head and clear my throat and twist my eyebrows until the hairs pirouetted like helicopter seeds. Yet the gremlin told me to do not-so-suffocating things, too. Things like spinning in the rain until the world smeared like watercolours, scaling beech trees despite my fear of heights, or disrobing and jumping in the inflatable pool on the playground, then investigating a shattered drainpipe. For the record, the school gave me an award for exposing *that* public health hazard. However, the accolade's name—the "Nudie Beauty" award—somewhat undermined its resumé potential.[2]

I breathed adventure, ticking and ticcing toward my next discovery like a neurotic Indiana Jones. No matter how many times I lost my path, the chatter of my compulsions and curiosities followed me through the maze. A constant, if unsolicited, companion in exploration.

The DSM-V classifies Tourette's as a tic "disorder," a problem requiring treatment. Something broken. Something not-quite-right. Something you can pinch and tuck and drown in Xanax and proclaim "all better!"

At the appointment with Dr. McGoogan, he and my parents carefully floated words toward each other like day-old helium balloons, stiffly volleying them as they trembled, hanging momentarily in the air. I glanced back at the sheet, turning *Tourette's* over on my tongue. *Tourette.* It tasted French, and I liked it. I also liked that it contained the word "tour" because a tour promised an adventure: an old-smelling art gallery, a rain-scented path through a tangle of beech trees, or, best of all, a library with a twisty staircase like the one in *Beauty and the Beast.* I lived for labyrinths of books: sometimes I was Theseus, sometimes I was Daedalus, but always I was David Bowie, magic-dancing my way through the stacks.

---

2 I tried slipping the award onto my college application before the school counsellor shut me down. Honestly, I'm more proud of this achievement than any other, including the time I ate nine saltines in one minute without water. That's three-quarters of a world record.

However, not all magic twirls through tangled bookshelves or sings in the rain and sparkles like fairy dust or releases chart-topping reggae fusion singles.[3] The voice in my head *is* my curse.

I felt like Aurora in *Sleeping Beauty*: bewitched at birth to prick my finger on a spinning wheel. Only, I would do it again and again and again and again. This curse lurked in my DNA, incurable by kiss (true love's or otherwise) or prescription. I wondered if a demon lived inside me. The Catholic officiaries in my community did not help to ease these suspicions, instead reprimanding me for asking too many questions in Sunday school[4] and for repeatedly clearing my throat during Communion. I became a disciple of loneliness, resigned to my labyrinth with only a friendly, twitching demon by my side.

There's a saying that goes something like, "You are never so alone as in a crowd." I don't know who said it. Maybe I did. Tourette's has a way of making you feel alone, like you're onstage squinting through the spotlights at an audience that won't even look you in the eye. When I tic in church, I am alone. When I tic at school, I am alone. When I tic at the supermarket or the committee meeting or the hardware store, the library or the parking lot or the elevator, the soccer game or the Christmas party or Carnegie Hall, I am all alone. Then I feel the kind of lost that makes me hug my knees under the nightshade, or where the path lies before me, all bright and alive, but you just stare, stare, stare. The kind of lost where I don't want to be found. So I discovered ways to lose myself.

I learned that when I funnel all my focus into an activity, the tics lessen. The voice in my head does not go entirely mum, but it quiets, stills, listens. When I sing, the demon nods its head to the beat.

When I write, my fingers dance and twitch about the computer keyboard like a glitching Franz Liszt.[5] When I run, my legs windmill

---

3 Fun fact: the band Magic! recently joined Samantha Bee, Kiefer Sutherland, and Alex Trebek on my running list of "Canadian Celebrities Whose Nationality I Was Surprised to Discover Because of My American Egocentrism."

4 I'd ask them things like "If Noah's ark landed in ancient Mesopotamia after Pangea fractured, then how did wallabies get to Australia?" The answer, of course, is that wallabies made a pact with Satan to join the pantheon of demons now running free in the Australian Outback. The Wallapocalypse is coming. Don't deny it, for deep down, you always knew it to be true.

5 Note to self: "Glitching Franz Liszt" isn't a bad band name.

in a familiar ticcing rhythm, the demon heaving and straining until it eventually falls into the pace. In those breezy moments, I am free.

Of course, exercising my creativity will not exorcise the voice in my head. I could sprint from Greensboro to Galilee[6] and Ol' Faithful Azazel[7] would be waiting for me at the finish line. I will never outrun my TS demons. All I can do is enter the labyrinth again and again, and Bowie knows it isn't a day outing. However, I've realized that the mutation in my DNA which condemns me to glitch like an infected Lenovo ThinkPad also instills in me an insatiable curiosity and obsessive drive to improve the world. Not to mention a proclivity for punning that may incite my brother to strangle me one day. I can't help but put some antics in semantics.[8] Like Harry Potter's psychic connection with Voldemort, my curse is also my greatest blessing. Except, unlike Harry, I can't innately speak to snakes. I had to take a class.[9]

One of two things I know for sure is that everyone is fighting something.[10] But in my extremely short time as a moderately successful human (if we measure success by the amount of peanut butter a person can consume in one sitting[11]), I find that the worst of the human experience can bring out the best of human ingenuity. I accept that the voice in my head is here to stay and, more importantly, that I don't want it to leave. I'm rather attached to it. Besides, it gets lonely in the labyrinth. It's nice to have the Minotaur (or, mino*tourette*?) for company.

When I say that getting lost is my greatest gift, I usually receive a dismissive waving of hands. *Nice try,* people say. *Your inability to*

---

6 Note to self: "Greensboro to Galilee" is a better band name.

7 Note to self: "Ol' Faithful Azazel" is the best band name.

8 Upon reading that sentence, my dear brother dropped the pages of this essay on the floor and walked away. I guess you could call it a death sentence.

9 Jest notwithstanding, four-year-old me really did want to become a snake charmer in Cairo for its cool mummies and cheap real estate.

10 The other thing I know for sure is that oatmeal raisin cookies were obviously created by the Communist Party of the Soviet Union during the Cold War to lower American morale. They look like chocolate chip cookies and taste like trust issues, and that's a fact.

11 I'm up to a respectable 1.4 midsize jars, which roughly translates to 25 ounces or 739 millilitres. Please hold your applause.

*locate your living room without Google Maps*[12] *is not a superpower.* But the subtle art of losing yourself is just that—an art, the product of excess creative energy that can be channelled through piano-playing, marathon-running, poetry-writing, opera-singing, and the occasional drainpipe misadventure. "Disorder" implies "wrong," but there is no *right* way to be. Heredity gave me a reservoir of nervous energy, and rather than dulling it with dams and Dexedrine, I run faster, write longer, sing higher, and am kinder. I create the energy away. The alleles that urge me to touchthefloortouchthefloortouchthefloor also afford me laser-like focus, letting me lose myself in letters, people, paintings, winding woods, and twisty staircases. I get lost to find myself and to live with the self I find. The tics and twitches are me just as my near-matrimonial devotion to Justin's Chocolate Hazelnut Butter is me, or my passion for making academic rap videos is me, or my use of the vocative comma in email greetings is me, or my desire to befriend both Oscar Wilde and Ernest Hemingway so I can make jokes about "the importance of being Ernest"[13] is me. I do not succeed despite my condition; I succeed[14] because of it, and to mute it is to blunt my creativity, my curiosity, my identity itself.

So when Dr. McGoogan drifted a stale red balloon with an "Rx" scribbled behind a boldfaced question mark, my mom stood, plucked the question mark out of the air, and squeezed. It popped with a flat crack and she flicked it onto the floor. As she strode toward the door, tugging my dad along, she paused. Turned. Smiled.

"Let's go," she said.

And for once in my life, I obeyed.

From then, we knew the first time I got stuck in a broken drainpipe would not be the last. I would walk into the labyrinth again and again, a restless adventurer getting lost, trying and testing and ticcing all while knowing I don't want to get out, that all I can do is stand at the

---

12 This joke is uncomfortably close to the truth. It's hard to overstate the extent of my navigational incapacity.

13 This zinger has been stewing in my head for two years and change. The only problem is, there are, by my calculations, approximately zero situations that would warrant its public appearance. Darn.

14 Again, assuming success is positively correlated with nut butter consumption. Which it obviously is.

crossroads of "was" and "will be" and explore the maze of being me, diagnosis and all. If I would end up being wrong, at least I would always be myself. That's the only life I would ever want to live.

Now, if you'll excuse me, I need to find my way down from this tree.

# Acknowledgements

Jennifer Lee Rossman's "The Falling Marionette" was previously published in *Expanded Horizons* in 2017 and *(Dis)ability* in 2018.

Susan Mockler's "Walking Class" was previously published as "You Oughta Know" in *Wordgathering* 12(4) in December 2018.

Hannah Foulger's "Bed eight, the ER, 2am" was previously published in *Matrix Magazine* in 2016.

Fira's "Pill Poppers" was previously published in *Stoked Words: An Anthology of Queer Poetry from the Capturing Fire Slam & Summit* in 2018.

Alice Wong's "On Valentine's Day, Let's Recognize Why #AccessIsLove" was previously published on RootedInRights.org on February 14th, 2019.

Nina Fosati's "Spoons" was previously published in the *Indiana Voice Journal* in March 2016.

Alice Wong's "Valuing Activism of All Kinds" was previously published on RootedInRights.org on April 5th, 2017.

Nina Fosati's "Companions" was previously published in *Breath & Shadow* 13(3) in July 2016.

Isabella J. Mansfield's "Aisle Nine: Bottled Water, Juice, Clearance, Bible Verses, Unwanted Attention" was previously published in *The Hollows of Bone* in 2019 by Finishing Line Press.

Katie Danis' "Create it Away" was previously published in *Open Minds Quarterly* in Fall 2018 and on storyhouse.org.

# Contributor Biographies

### Ace Tilton Ratcliff

Ratcliff lives and works in sunny south Florida, surrounded by their pack of wild beasts and veterinarian husband. Their meatcage is infested with Ehlers-Danlos syndrome, dysautonomia, endometriosis, and a whole host of other comorbidities. They're a photographer, artist, former mortician, and freelance writer with bylines at *Huffington Post*, *io9*, *Bitch Media*, *Narratively*, *Catapult*, *Uncanny Magazine*, *Fireside Fiction*, and more. They co-own an in-home veterinary practice called Harper's Promise with their husband, focusing specifically on end-of-life care and euthanasia. When not creating, they're reading and sometimes tweeting at the same time @MortuaryReport.

### Aimee Louw

Louw is a queer, disabled poet, freelance writer, and media artist of British and Afrikaans-Canadian heritage. Her writing spans topics of Disability Justice, sexuality, undoing settler fantasies, and feminism. She directs the Underwater City Project, a zine series which explores living within normative infrastructures and shares visions of swimming to the nearest grocery store. Louw has contributed her poetry and non-fiction to CBC Radio, Canadaland, *GUTS* magazine, *The Geeky Gimp*, and *The Tempest*. She is currently working on her debut novel, *You Deserve Everything*.

### Alice Wong

Wong is a disability activist, media maker, and consultant. She is the Founder and Director of the Disability Visibility Project® created in 2014, an online community dedicated to creating, sharing, and amplifying Disability media and culture. Alice is also a co-partner in four projects: DisabledWriters.com, a resource to help editors connect with Disabled writers and journalists; #CripLit, a series of Twitter chats for Disabled writers with novelist Nicola Griffith; #CripTheVote, a nonpartisan online movement encouraging the political participation of Disabled people with Andrew Pulrang and Gregg Beratan; and Access Is Love with Mia Mingus and Sandy Ho, a campaign that aims to help build a world where accessibility is understood as an act of love instead of a burden or an afterthought.

## Bipin Kumar

A multidisciplinary artist from Brampton, Ontario, Kumar uses many forms of the arts to bring focus to mental health issues. Since 2017, Kumar has been writing about his own experiences with both physical and mental disability, having both ataxia and an undisclosed psychotic and/or manic mental illness. He uses his writing as a way to have open and honest communication with others about mental health, as well as learning about his own personality. He has started an arts initiative with other artists called Make It Mindful.

## Cathy Bryant

Hailing from Chesire, United Kingdom, Bryant is disabled and bisexual and she worked as a life model, shop assistant, civil servant, and childminder before becoming a professional writer. Bryant has won 27 literary awards, including the Bulwer-Lytton Fiction Prize and the Wergle Flomp Humor Poetry Contest. Her work has appeared in over 250 publications. She has published two books of poetry titled *Contains Strong Language and Scenes of a Sexual Nature* and *Look at All the Women*, and a how-to novel titled *How to Win Writing Competitions*. She co-edited the three volumes of *Best of Manchester Poets*, and her new collection titled *Erratics* is out now.

## Ciro di Ruocco

di Ruocco, who is both Canadian and American, is a visual artist who completed a BA of Visual Arts at Vancouver Island University in 2018. He is currently working on an MFA at Vermont College of Fine Arts. He has won many art and poetry awards, and has been published in various print publications.

## Deborah Chava Singer

Originally from San Diego, Singer studied with the Mesa College Theatre Company and Queer Players. While going to school in Toronto, she remembered what she really wanted most was to be a writer. She currently resides in Vancouver, Washington. Her writing has appeared in *Hashtag Queer* Vol 2, *Lemondead* zine, *The Santa Fe Literary Review*, *The Human Touch Journal*, *Cirque Journal*, *MUSE Magazine*, *The Chaffin Journal*, *Heart and Mind* zine,

*Snapdragon, Twisted Vine, Labletter, Off the Rocks, The Rockhurst Review, Trajectory,* and *Steam Ticket.* Her website is LateNightAwake. com.

## Diane Driedger
Driedger is a visual artist, poet, and educator. She is author and editor of six books about Disability. Her latest book *is Untold Stories: A Canadian Disability History Reader* (2018), co-edited with Nancy Hansen and Roy Hanes. Her book *Red with Living: Poems and Art* was published by Inanna in 2016. She is Assistant Professor in the Interdisciplinary Master's Program in Disability Studies at the University of Manitoba.

## Eryn Goodman
Currently living on Vancouver Island, Canada, Goodman lives with chronic lyme disease and has been a full-time wheelchair user since age 15. They love drawing and painting, often livestreaming current art projects. Their career goals include gaining a post-secondary fine arts education and becoming a tattoo artist.

## Fira
Fira (they/he) is a spoken word poet currently residing in Tkaronto (Toronto). His work focusses on the topics of mental health, queerness, and healing through art. His experience with mental illness has pushed him to write and perform to encourage others to tell their story and feel less alone. He has competed at the national level on poetry teams for Guelph and Burlington, as well as helped organize the national youth poetry festival, Voices of Today. He can most easily be found on Instagram @Fira_Astrali where he encourages you to reach out!

## Hannah Foulger
Foulger is a British-Canadian theatre artist and writer with a disability. Born in Amsterdam, she was raised in Cambridge, Ontario. In 2010, she endured a blood clot and brain haemorrhage. She is a graduate of English and Theatre at University of Winnipeg. Her work has appeared in *Prairie Fire, Matrix Magazine,* Sick+Twisted's *Lame Is...* cabaret, and

the Winnipeg Fringe Festival. She lives in Winnipeg with epilepsy, a brain injury, and a grey tabby named Frodo.

## Isabella J. Mansfield

Mansfield's poetry has been featured by *Philosophical Idiot*, *The Wild Word*, and *Sad Girl Review*. In 2017, she was Brittany Noakes Award semi-finalist. She won the 2018 Mark Ritzenhein New Author Award. Her chapbook, *The Hollows of Bone*, was released in 2019 by Finishing Line Press. She lives in Howell, Missouri with her husband and son.

## Jan Steckel

A former pediatrician who stopped practising medicine because of chronic pain, Steckel now has her latest poetry book, *Like Flesh Covers Bone*, published with Zeitgeist Press in 2018. Her poetry book, *The Horizontal Poet* (Zeitgeist Press, 2011) won a 2012 Lambda Literary Award. Her fiction chapbook *Mixing Tracks* (Gertrude Press, 2009) and poetry chapbook *The Underwater Hospital* (Zeitgeist Press, 2006) also received awards. Her fiction and poetry have appeared in *Scholastic Magazine*, *Bellevue Literary Review*, *New Verse News*, *November 3 Club*, *Assaracus*, and elsewhere. Her work has been nominated three times for a Pushcart Prize. She lives in Oakland, California.

## Jennifer Lee Rossman

Rossman is a writer and editor of speculative fiction. She is autistic and has spinal muscular atrophy. Her debut novel, *Jack Jetstark's Intergalactic Freakshow*, is now available from World Weaver Press and she is currently writing a book about Disabled werewolves. She blogs at jenniferleerossman.blogspot.com and tweets @JenLRossman.

## Jessi Eoin

Eoin is a multiply-disabled, chronically ill, agender artist living on Lenape and Canarsie land known as Brooklyn, New York. Eoin loves all things cozy, witchy, and nature-related and include these elements in their work in hopes of making viewers feel at home in their body and spirit. They share more about themself and their work at their website JBeoin.com.

## Jill M. Talbot

Talbot's writing has appeared in *The Fiddlehead, Geist, Rattle, PRISM, The Stinging Fly*, and others. Jill won the PRISM Grouse Grind Lit Prize, and she was shortlisted for the Matrix Lit POP Award and the Malahat Far Horizons Award. Talbot lives in Vancouver, Canada.

## K. Bron Johnson

Johnson is an #ActuallyAutistic late-diagnosed adult living in Montreal. Recently diagnosed with otosclerosis as well, she advocates for herself and other multiply-Disabled people through her consultancy business, Completely Inclusive. As a biracial woman, her writing often touches on the intersection of race, disability, and feminist issues. She has contributed to *All the Weight of Our Dreams: On Living Racialized Autism* and *Knowing Why: Adult-Diagnosed Autistic People on Life and Autism*.

## Kate Grisim

Grisim has been reading her whole life and, at some point, she started writing about it too. She graduated with her Master's of Arts in Disability Studies from the University of Manitoba in 2018. Her thesis was on how she read as a young, newly-disabled child on the school bus every day and how the literature helped her embrace a disabled identity. She is the co-editor of an online magazine called *Exoplanet* which publishes stories of diverse speculative fiction, sci-fi, and fantasy. She is on Twitter @KateGrisim.

## Katie Danis

Danis runs the research and commentary blog ProbablyLostKatie. wordpress.com. Her work has been published in *Open Minds Quarterly*, and she is a student at the University of North Carolina at Chapel Hill.

## Kimberley Hunter

Hunter is a Creative Writing and History student at Vancouver Island University in Nanaimo, Canada. She was officially diagnosed with Asperger's syndrome at age 20. She has one poem published in *Navigator Student Press*, and hopes to write and publish novels.

## Lara Ameen

Ameen is a Disability Studies PhD student at Chapman University. She received an MFA in Screenwriting from California State University, Northridge, and a BA in Film Studies with a minor in Disability Studies from UC Berkeley. Her scripts have placed in Screencraft's Bahamas Screenwriters Residency Program, Austin Film Festival Screenplay Competition, and Fresh Voices Screenplay Competition. She is a 2018 recipient of the NBC Universal Tony Coelho Media Scholarship. Passionate about intersectional Disability representation, she hopes to publish a series of fantasy novels and become a showrunner for a supernatural TV drama series featuring queer Disabled characters.

## Leah Lakshmi Piepzna-Samarasinha

Leah is a queer disabled femme writer and disability justice movement worker of Burgher/Tamil Sri Lankan and Irish/Roma ascent. The Lambda award-winning author of *Tonguebreaker, Care Work: Dreaming Disability Justice, Dirty River: A Queer Femme of Color Dreaming Her Way Home, Bodymap, Love Cake,* and *Consensual Genocide,* and co-editor of *The Revolution Starts At Home: Confronting Intimate Violence in Activist Communities,* they *are a* lead artist with Disability Justice performance collective Sins Invalid. Her writing has been widely published, with recent work in *PBS Newshour,* Poets.org's *Poetry and the Body, The Deaf Poets Society, Bitch, Self, TruthOut,* and *The Body is Not an Apology.* She is a VONA Fellow and holds an MFA from Mills College. She is also a rust belt poet, a Sri Lankan with a white mom, a femme over 40, a grassroots intellectual, a survivor who is hard to kill.

## Lys Morton

Morton lives in Nanaimo, Canada, and is currently in his final year at Vancouver Island University for a BA in Creative Writing. He's Associate Editor at *Navigator Student Press,* where various articles of his have been published. His work has also been featured at *The Coil* and he was the 2018 winner of the Mike Matthews Humorous Essay Award. You can follow his work at Facebook.com/LysWritesNow.

## Marrok Zenon Sedgwick
A disabled trans activist and educator, Sedgwick uses art as his primary tool for challenging society's injustices. Working as a creative producer and documentarian, Sedgwick seeks to centralize the stories of Deaf and Disabled people, especially those whose identities intersect with the LGBTQIA+ community. Sedgwick's research interests include disability studies and queer/sexuality studies, and has recently been developing a dramaturgical process for universal design for performance/media. His writing has previously been published in Autonomous Press' *Spoon Knife 2*.

## Michaela Oteri
Otherwise known as Ogrefairy, Oteri is a 29-year-old disabled digital artist who has Ehlers-Danlos syndrome. She has been working on her Cripple Punk Portrait Series since 2016. Oteri's work has been featured by the Deaf Poet's Society and she is published in *Loosely Speaking: An Anthology of Life with Elhers-Danlos Syndrome*. Her work was also displayed in Washington, DC for Rare Disease Week 2019.

## Niamh Timmons
Timmons is a queer disabled crazy non-binary Transwoman. Her writings frequently engage the intersections of Disability, transness, mental health, and survivorhood. They've been established on *The Establishment* and profiled on *Autostraddle* and *Buzzfeed*. She does a variety of performance art, zine-making, bad comics, and other writing they barely have energy for. They currently live on occupied Kalapuya lands. You can find her on Twitter @CallMeAmab.

## Nicola Kapron
Kapron has been writing for as long as she can remember, even when it was physically painful. She has been diagnosed with faceblindness, coding difficulties, dysgraphia, and topographagnosia. She works on independent video games or sews stuffed animals in her spare time. She currently lives in British Columbia, Canada.

## Nina Fosati
Fosati is an artist by inclination and a writer by misfortune. Most recently, idiopathic peripheral neuropathy earned her an accessible

parking hangtag and a card-carrying claim to being Disabled. Links to her stories can be found on her website NinaFosati.com, or follow her on Twitter @NinaFosati.

## Rebecca Johnson

Born with arthrogryposis multiplex congenita, Johnson has lived in Dothan, Alabama all her life and is a wheelchair user. She currently teaches US History and University Orientation at Troy University and Kingdom College. She also works as a student advisor and disability services coordinate at Troy University.

## Susan Mockler

Mockler is a psychologist living in Kingston, Ontario. Her fiction and non-fiction have appeared in *THIS Magazine, Geist, Wordgathering, Ars Medica, Descant*, and *Taddle Creek*. She has recently completed a memoir describing her experiences recovering from a spinal cord injury from which her contribution in this book is excerpted.

# About the Editor

sb. smith is a queer Disabled writer, editor, artist, and cat lover living on Musqueam, Squamish and Tsleil-Waututh land (known as Vancouver). She is a student of creative writing and sociology at Vancouver Island University and their own writing has been published in *antilang., Rooted in Rights, Portal, Sad Girl Review, Navigator Student Press*, and more. She is dedicated to Disability Justice initiatives by helping amplify diverse Disabled voices through both their professional and community-based work.

# OTHER ANTHOLOGIES BY REBEL MOUNTAIN PRESS

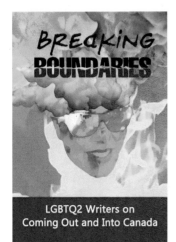

*Breaking Boundaries:*
*LGBTQ2 Writers on Coming Out and Into Canada*

ISBN: 978-0-9947302-7-5 |Paperback: 6x9, 146 pp, $13.95

An anthology of short-stories, memoirs, and poetry by LGBTQ2 writers across Canada (Canada-born, immigrated, or refugee). The common thread throughout is that for LGBTQ2 people, Canada is the place to be. Nominated for the 2019 GEORGE RYGA AWARD for social awareness.

*"What does it mean to be LGBTQ2 in Canada? The only possible answer to that question is one given in many voices . . . There is struggle in these stories and poems, but there is also strength and resilience, compassion and determination,"* from foreword by Robin Stevenson, author of *Pride: Celebrating Diversity and Community*

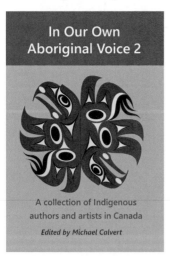

*In Our Own Aboriginal Voice 2:*
*A collection of Indigenous authors and artists in Canada*

Editor: Michael Calvert
ISBN: 978-1-7753019-1-2 |Paperback: 6x9, 148 pp, $18.95

A collection Indigenous writing by established authors such as the late Connie Fife, Joanne Arnott, Michelle Sylliboy, and Dennis Saddleman, and other emerging Indigenous writers from across Canada.

*"These voices are precious and beautiful. Mahsi cho to each of them singing the world to a brighter place. Mahsi cho to their ancestors and mahsi cho to a richer world because of their courage and bravery."* ~Richard Van Camp, author of *Moccasin Square Gardens*